THE

PRISONERS OF ST.-LAZARE.

BY

MADAME * * * *,

EDITED BY

MME. PAULINE DE GRANDPRÉ.

TRANSLATED FROM THE FRENCH BY

MRS. E. M. McCARTHY.

NEW YORK:
D. APPLETON & COMPANY,
549 & 551 BROADWAY.
1872.

EDITOR'S PREFACE.

The manuscript of this work was left me by a dear friend, now deceased, and who died before reaching her thirtieth year. You who may read these lines, study well the matter she places before you. It was gathered by her almost on the verge of the tomb. Mày the living seek to profit by the experience of those who have gone before!

Although the work has been written with all the reserve a matter so delicate requires, it is not one to be placed indiscriminately in the hands of young girls. But all mothers should read it, and all young girls who have lost their mothers.

Pauline de Grandpré.

Paris.

TRANSLATOR'S PREFACE.

The evils that fester within the bosom of French society may have peculiar features of their own, but it cannot be denied that there is at least sufficient parity in the state of affairs here to make this book useful to the American public. The remedies it suggests for some of these evils are certainly worth considering. Society owes it to itself to shield the honest poor, especially those of the weaker sex, from the dangers to which destitution exposes them, and to do so in a way that will not wound a just pride. It ought to protect those who, once unfortunate, desire to return to the paths of virtue and honor.

In the incarceration of women for transgressions of the law, moral reformation, more than merely vindictive punishment, should be the object kept in view. This is to be accomplished not by obtrusive measures, not by violating the religious freedom of the prisoner, but by means and opportunities ever present and ever accessible to her, by which conscience may be awakened, or directed when awakened, and a path made clear by which she may escape a life of ignominy. We take St.-Lazaro, so far as this book gives us an insight into its discipline, to be a prison managed with this view of reforming quite as much as of punishing its inmates. What it chiefly needs to make it more effective is the supplementary institution referred to in the appendix. The interior administration of this prison appears to be in the hands of women entirely devoted to their work from religious motives, and carrying the best of influences into the discharge of their duties, whether as custodians, as industrial superintendents, or as kind counsellors.

Desiring to do homage to the nobility of purpose which evidently animated the authoress, the translator has availed herself of her scanty leisure to put the work in an English dress, hoping that it may thus be rendered more accessible to the many good and noble men and women who interest themselves in behalf of the unfortunate. The dramatic cast given to some portions of the book will not perhaps be in accord with the tastes of those who will read it in its English version, and they might be tempted to set it aside on this account as in some degree sensational. We beg to remind them, however, that the book is written by a Frenchwoman, and addressed to the tastes of those of her own nation, while honestly seeking to enlist their sympathy and attention in behalf of the suffering or the tempted of her sex. To adapt it the better to the end it is to serve among its present readers, some superfluities in the original have been retrenched.

It was the desire of Mdlle. Grandpré that the work should be translated in this country, and that any profits that might accrue from the publication should be devoted to the undertaking she has in hand, or had, previous to the terrible misfortunes that have fallen upon Paris, the Asylum for the Discharged Prisoners of St.-Lazare ("Œuvre des Liberées de Saint-Lazare"). It is the intention of the translator to coöperate in this wish of Mdlle. Grandpré.

SYRACUSE, N. Y., *April*, 1871.

THE

PRISONERS OF ST.-LAZARE.

August 1, 1865.

DEAR MARIE: I promised you an account of my impressions during my sojourn at "St.-Lazare," and, to assure you of the approaching fulfilment of that promise, I announce that I have arrived, and that my first thought is of you.

I am in my chamber, writing to you upon a little table placed before a window which overlooks the court-yard of the prison. What sad but salutary reflections crowd upon the mind! There are before me a multitude of women, some guilty, all unfortunate. Many are condemned justly, and certainly all are condemned by public opinion. Soon I shall be permitted a nearer view to study them, to listen to them, and, perhaps, to console them.

Marie, why are you not with me—you, whose voice is so sweet, whose glance is so sympathetic, and whose heart is so good — you, who would know much better than I how to dry their tears? You, whose mind is so elevated, could comprehend them better, and, gathering up their confessions, draw from them suitable instruction for others.

Although I may not have your superior intelligence, nor possess your rare soul, dear Marie, I will listen, I will observe, and will convey to you all my impressions, both cheering and saddening. You will answer me, and we shall perpetuate the union of our early youth, when, with our hearts upon our lips, we walked hand-in-hand, enjoying together the perfume of the flowers, and the refreshing coolness of the breezes.

It was only last evening that I reached the prison. The journey was a long one, and, overcome by fatigue, I fell asleep in the carriage. I was suddenly awakened from my uneasy slumbers by the abrupt stoppage of my vehicle, and the hasty opening of the door, with the announcement by the coachman, "Here we are, madame." While my baggage was being unloaded, I cast a frightened glance upon the façade of my new dwelling; but, as the night was dark, the street-light afforded me only an imperfect view of a mass of gray stone. An armed sentry, on guard, stood motionless in the angle of the gate-way. An indescribable sadness came over me as if, on crossing the threshold, I were about to renounce my liberty. I hazarded a light stroke of the knocker, and the porter turned the heavy lock with a loud noise.

"What do you wish, madame?"

"I wish to see M. X.," said I.

"Very well, madame; such a floor and such a door."

The corridor was large, the stairs were wide, and, as I slowly mounted them, beloved friends gathered around me, pressing my hand in joyful welcome, and leading me in. On entering the parlor I accidentally caught a glimpse of my face in the mirror. I was pale, and could but smile at my frightened look; however, I was quickly reassured by seeing the pleasure that my arrival had caused. We ate, we talked, and finally, when on retiring I threw myself upon the bed, I forgot the prison and its inmates.

I awoke this morning, overcome by fatigue, and lay in a semi-conscious state between dreaming and waking, startled at intervals by loud voices. When I opened my eyes it was with difficulty that I could discern the objects that surrounded me. My curtains were carefully closed, and scarcely a ray of light was permitted to enter my chamber. Suddenly I remembered that I was in "St.-Lazare." I arose from my bed, and, hastily throwing on a dressing-gown, drew aside my bed-curtains, and repaired to the window. Looking down, I beheld the inmates of St.-Lazare, or, at least, that portion of them who enjoy the privilege of a recreation in the morning. It was their voices that had aided to awaken me.

The first court-yard (*la première cour*) of St.-Lazare is very spacious, and is divided in two by a high wall, rising to the height of the first story. One part, which is paved and inaccessible to the inmates, is appropriated entirely to the carriages which bring hither daily so many unhappy ones. The other portion is planted with trees of tolerable size, with leaves of a sickly green. One would suppose that the sun never visited them, and that they were watered with tears.

You know how much I love fine trees and verdure; well, it may be strange, but here these objects inspire no cheerfulness; they rather sadden me. Can it be possible for the wind ever to circulate among their stunted branches? No; they are without life, without air. Like the poor inmates whom they shelter, one might imagine even that they wanted liberty. This place is full of interest. Trees, buildings, every thing, I shall examine narrowly, but especially the inmates, of whom, as yet, I know nothing.

August 2d.

My second night at St.-Lazare has been a strangely agitated one. I was no longer fatigued as on the preceding night, and the slightest noise was sufficient to arouse me. I heard almost every quarter sounded by the great clock in the middle of the court-yard.

I arose while yet the street-light threw its ominous reflection upon numerous windows, garnished by bars of iron. I do not know why I was afraid, but I crouched in my bed, concealing my head under the covering, finally falling asleep. The most fantastic dreams visited me. Undoubtedly one sleeps badly in prison, even with a tranquil conscience. This morning my friends laugh at my fears of the past night. I desired to go out that I might persuade myself of the fact that I was free, and, as I presented myself at the outer door, the keeper stepped suddenly before me, and, looking at me for a moment with an air of suspicion, said:

"What do you wish, madame?"

"Sir," I replied, "will you have the kindness to open the door?"

He hesitated still, then suddenly striking his forehead, pulled off his cap with a lively movement, and said to me:

"I recognize you now, madame; you are the person who came here the day before yesterday; you can pass, madame."

He then turned his great key in the heavy lock, and I stood outside. He had taken me at first for one of the inmates endeavoring to escape. I inquired how those who lived there until their term of sentence had expired were set free, and found that for the inmates of the first section it was very simple. A card is given to each one, on which is written the word "Liberty," which she presents to the keeper at the door. It was this passport that he awaited from me, and that, as you can readily imagine, I was not prepared to give him. Formerly a superintendent accompanied the liberated person to the door and pronounced the word "Liberty," and this magic word sufficed to open the door to the inmates of this section of St.-Lazare. As to those of the second and third sections, they are liberated only at the *préfecture.*

August 3d.

How vast these corridors are, dear Marie, on which the cells of the inmates open to the right and left! I cannot give you an exact description of them to-day; I will enter upon details as they shall naturally present themselves.

The prisoners are distributed among three sections: the first contains those under arrest, or who have been already tried; the second is composed of depraved women; and the third of young girls sent for correction. They all wear a uniform, consisting of a gown of coarse woollen stuff—brown, blue, or gray, according to the section to which they belong—and a light-blue cape, with a cap of cloth. This costume is neither elegant nor poetic, and, indeed, strikes one at once as being decidedly ugly.

August 4th.

I am sad and I feel unwell; it is cloudy, and will rain perhaps. I have not left my room to-day, and my only distraction has been to observe the inmates. Poor women! whatever their faults may be, however low they may have fallen, I feel for them an immeasurable pity. At the hour of recreation they pass into the court like shadows, and are obliged to speak in a subdued tone of voice. No sound reaches my ear, although so little space separates us. The greater part remain seated on the benches, while the rest walk slowly around. I do not know to what section these belong.

When the young girls of the department of correction take their recreation, there is much noise and running about, but the others are more grave, because they have suffered more. Some of the religious are always with them. What a contrast! The sisters are calm and serene, and their presence produces a good influence. They live amid the victims of every vice, of every passion, and of every kind of misery, yet nothing affects or agitates them; they resemble a rock placed in the midst of the billows, which, beaten by the waves, remains immovable, and braves the fury of every tempest. The religious wear habits of black serge, and upon the head a triple veil—one of white cambric, the other two of woollen material, one blue, the other black. The hair and part of the forehead are entirely concealed by a white band. A circular cape, made of white linen, like the band, covers the shoulders, a crucifix is suspended round the neck, and a rosary, attached to the belt, hangs at the side.

These women, admirable for their simplicity, are happy in their sublime vocation, and are uniformly cheerful. In the infirmary, devoted nurses; in the workshops, vigilant guardians; they devote themselves to these unhappy ones, instructing, consoling, and watching over them, and doing all without effort and without disgust. The labors of their exile do not weary them, for their kingdom is not of this world. They are beloved as well as respected: to convince you of this, it is sufficient to say that fifty religious hold in perfect discipline twelve hundred inmates—twelve hundred women!

The sisters of the prison have their mother-house near Limoges. The congregation was instituted less than twenty-five years ago; little by little it has extended itself, until now it serves almost all the prisons of France. They are called the "Sisters of Marie-Joseph."

But of what importance is the name, whether known as "Sisters of St. Vincent de Paul," "Little Sisters of the Poor," or "Sisters of Marie-Joseph?" All belong to that great family Christianity has given birth to for the consolation of sorrowing humanity.

This Christian family, the refuge of the sick, the support of orphans, the consolation of the miserable everywhere—this family, indispensable to our hospitals and prisons, France, our dear country, is justly proud of, as lending additional lustre to her glory. In the presence of its members, the impious themselves are restrained: in the same breath with which the latter proclaim "Defiance to Almighty God," they exclaim "All honor to the sisters!". . . . But Marie, I must pause. The thought of the sisters has so engrossed me that I have forgotten my prisoners. . . .

"What has brought all these women to St.-Lazare?" you will ask.—Ah! what a mournful variety of miseries!—But, you ask me, have all these women arrived at the same goal by the same course? Are they all women of the lowest grade in life? No, all the vices of civilization, all ranks of society, are represented here. But are all alike perverse, vicious, and depraved? Again, no. Let me relate to you the case of one as described to me by the Mother-Assistant:

A young girl of fourteen is arrested by the police as a vagrant, and sent to St.-Lazare. Her exterior is prepossessing. She is questioned. The poor child cannot read; she has been baptized, perhaps, but has never made her first communion, nor has she even ever heard of God, nor been taught any ideas of morality. Her parents led bad lives and her life has been like theirs.

Here she is instructed, spoken to of heaven, of her soul, and of the dignity that belongs to woman; she has been taught her duties toward God, toward society, toward herself, and there have been gradually revealed, in this poor, abandoned girl, all the best traits of mind and heart. She has become an example to her companions, has the piety of an angel, is constant in labor, and full of gratitude to the sisters.

One night the religious who was on duty, on visiting her cell, found her sleeping upon the boards of her little bed, enveloped in a large, coarse, brown woollen spread, having removed the mattresses. As she was sleeping soundly, the sister did not awaken her, but the next day she was questioned by the superior, when she confessed that she was imposing upon herself this penance, hoping thereby to obtain from Heaven the conversion of her father and mother. Poor child!—She no longer harbored the remembrance that her father had often beaten her, and that her mother had refused her bread and shelter.

Dear Marie, I cannot refrain from making a few reflections upon our own lives. Had we been reared as this girl has been, what would have been our destiny? God, on the contrary, placed us in the bosom of honorable families, where we beheld only the best examples. The women of our families were pure, and the men uncorrupted; we were born far from the poisonous atmosphere of large cities; we lived in the wholesome open air, like two shrubs, healthy and vigorous; and, to counteract any rusticity of manners that might be engendered by our country-life, we had thrown around our childhood the charm, the perfume, the poetry of religion. Do you not remember the flowers we used to gather in the park and carry to the village church, where our mothers taught us to arrange them with our own hands? You will also remember those rustic processions which wound their way over the fields, or beneath the trees which overshadowed the paths, and how their white banners fluttered in the breeze! How devout were the hymns of the peasants, how sweet the voices of the priests! How often, with tears of devotion, we knelt to implore the protection of the saints, bending reverently before their shrines!

Our mothers restrained our wayward inclinations, and developed the germs of all that was good in us. Your disposition was amiable, and care was taken to fortify you against its excesses; my nature was a proud one, and it was moulded into dignity. It is expected of us now, therefore, that we should fulfil great duties, for from "those who have received much, much will be required."

August 5th.

In our day, dear Marie, the character, the varied dispositions, and the wants of woman, are an all-engrossing subject. Some depreciate and others extol her; perhaps no one knows her thoroughly. Her nature is a profound one, and not easily fathomed. She is sometimes sublimely disinterested, at others absurdly selfish; she is a being engrossed in many cares, full of whims and caprices, perhaps, but no less so of charms and sweetnesses; sometimes rising to the height of energy and self-devotion, and again as weak as an infant. Inspired with enthusiasm, she becomes even stronger than man. Her character, then, is a legitimate object of study, for, upon this many-sided creature depend, in a great degree, the happiness and security of society.

Man has in vain endeavored to study woman; the subject baffles him; he finds it difficult to understand her. It is necessary to be a woman, in order to paint all the shades of woman's character, to throw light upon all the recesses of her heart, to account for the vacillations that are peculiar to her, to reveal the motives of the joy or of the sorrow that make up her existence. But of what value will be even the most conscentious study?—how sterile in results must it be, if it have not for its object to provide a stimulus for her virtues, and an antidote for her faults!

Pardon me, Marie, for these digressions, in which from time to time I shall presume to indulge. I feel sure of your approval, and I am also sure that you sympathize with my subject, and that, to one of the best of women, a topic that concerns her sex cannot be a matter of indifference.

10 *o'clock in the evening.*

All the inmates are sleeping; what silence! How calm is every thing about me; no sounds but the monotonous song of the cricket, and the distant rumbling of carriages in noisy Paris! The sky is so clear; the stars twinkle in myriads, and the moon shines down into the court-yard upon the motionless trees. On all the inmates the bolts are securely drawn.

Unfortunate women, what visions occupy them? They dream, perhaps, of liberty, or they return to the home of their childhood, a wretched hovel it may be, covered with moss, the fire shining upon the hearth, the grandmother at the spinning-wheel, the children grouped around the father, who relates legends of former days. Happy hours, when they could sleep peacefully on their straw couch, when remorse and suffering, sin and sorrow, were unknown! Alas! sin and sorrow stand now by the cot of this poor prisoner, and only await her awakening to be recognized! Sleep on, then, unhappy ones, over whose souls sin has breathed its poisonous miasma. To-morrow you will awake to another day of expiation. Repentance effaces crime, and God pardons, but society never forgets!

Midnight.

I have written little, dear friend, but I have thought much. Midnight sounds from that great clock which measures time with frightful rapidity; midnight! the hour when tombs open, and the dead return to visit the homes that knew them in life. Ah! if all the dead of St.-Lazare could return to life, what a mournful procession of phantoms should we behold! Those pale spectres were, when living, the opprobrium of society, but, dying, they departed in the peace of heaven; for over their heads the Christian priest raised his consecrated hands, and reconciled them to God.—*Requiescant in pace!*

August 6th, 4 o'clock in the morning.

I threw myself upon the bed, but without the power to rest. I slept a few hours, but my sleep was disturbed.

Four o'clock, and the little birds are already awake and begin to sing; with what joyous notes they salute the opening day! They are at liberty, these little birds; they come from choice to eat the bread of the prisoners, but they can also fly rapidly away, for space is free to them.

Five o'clock.

The religious have already risen; the clock has called them to the chapel to say the "Angelus." I will go to pray with them. . . . Dear Marie, I have prayed for you, for all I love, and for all who suffer. Prayer is, for woman above all, consolation and strength; and, when offered to God in the early morning, raises the soul on high, and insures a day of purity and calm.

August 7th.

One of the saddest emotions I experience here is occasioned by the arrival of the prison-vans, which stop just under my window. They have something ominous in their rumble; the keepers gather in the court, the turnkey opens the door, and these unfortunate females descend and enter the prison-gate. Some, dressed in startling toilets, descend laughingly from the dismal carriage; others, clad more simply, cross the threshold of St.-Lazare with a calm and dignified step; but far the greater number wear tattered and disordered garments, the livery of idleness and dissipation.

There has just arrived an old woman who, with much difficulty, totters along, supported by her cane, and a young child of ten years, the latter found homeless and abandoned in the streets of Paris. How the spectacle grieves my heart!

A few days ago a young woman, in the flower of her age, was brought here, dying of exhaustion from hunger; she was so feeble that the keepers were obliged to carry her, and she was as pale as a corpse. For her, succor came too late; she had suffered too long, and she died of weakness. Misery is always heart-rending, but when one is brought to it by vice it is frightful! and this is the fate of the greater part of dissolute women. These poor creatures consume their youth in a few foolish and tempestuous joys; and, at the age when other women have arrived at the full bloom of life, these are jaded and worn out, and are fast hastening to the grave.

August 8th.

The name of "St.-Lazare" inspires terror; it is a tigma of infamy, for it is popularly believed that this house is a refuge only for women of bad repute. This is an error. There are females committed here for slight offences, and some may even be guiltless of the charges alleged against them; but, innocent or guilty, all the inmates will carry with them through life the stigma of having been committed to "St.-Lazare."

The reputation of a woman resembles a delicate flower, that the least impure breath can tarnish forever. It is not sufficient to be virtuous only, it is necessary also never to have been suspected.

August 9th.

The weather is warm, the sky is clear, and the sun is dazzling. You should hear my swallows chirp! The window of the work-room looks out upon a little court where some lovely little messengers of spring are building their nests. I call this the "Court of Swallows," because I never see any other species of bird in it. When I am tired of writing, I draw aside my white curtains and listen to the chattering of my graceful, black-winged neighbors. I watch their little pastimes, and see them make their evolutions around the nests of their young. From this court also, the songs of some of the inmates reach my ear; they sing at certain hours the hymns that the religious teach them, and sing in perfect harmony. This music, although from feeble throats, breaks agreeably the silence of the prison, and is very moving, especially when we call to mind that the voices we hear are those chiefly of young girls from whose lips were formerly heard only the accents of mad revelry. They also accompany the organ in the chapel, which is played by one of the religious. It is touching to listen to them; their voices move *our* hearts; why may they not also move the heart of *God?*

HISTORICAL SKETCH OF ST.-LAZARE.

St.-Lazare occupies the site of an ancient abbey destroyed by the Normans in 885, but the origin of which is lost in the night of ages. On its ruins a hospital was established for the reception of the numerous victims of Eastern leprosy among the ranks of the returned Crusaders. Hence the name, "St.-Lazare," St. Lazarus being regarded as the patron saint of lepers. As a hospital, it was served by monks and nuns of the Augustinian order. The kings of the third French race frequently visited it. In fact, one portion of the house bore the title of "*Logis du Roi.*" Kings and queens, at the beginning of their reign, were accustomed to spend twenty days here. After their death, the royal remains were deposited for a time at St.-Lazare, where the funeral absolution was given before their removal to the vaults of St.-Denis.

In 1632 St. Vincent de Paul established here his congregation, the Lazarists, so called from the place of their origin. Sick and insane patients were then received, as well as lepers. The establishment was at once a hospital, a seminary, and a convent, and ecclesiastics came here to make retreats. The great Bossuet himself here prepared for ordination, and the walls of St.-Lazare frequently afterward re-echoed to his eloquence.

After long continuing the scene of the admirable charities of St. Vincent de Paul and his successors, the Revolution of 1789 came, and the house was pillaged. More than four hundred of the assailants perished on this occasion, chiefly by drinking themselves to death in the cellars, or by poisoning themselves with the articles found in the pharmacy. The place was gutted, and the admirable paintings which adorned the refectory were carried off. St.-Lazare then became a prison.

In 1848 its gates were opened, and the greater part of the prisoners set free. The national workshops were then established on the ground-floor, where those of the untried prisoners (*détenues*) now are.

In 1850 the cell formerly occupied by St. Vincent de Paul was erected into a chapel by Monseigneur Sibour, Archbishop of Paris, as an inscription in its sacristy testifies.

THE HOUSE OF ST.-LAZARE.

THE house of St.-Lazare is built in the form of a parallelogram, about four hundred and eighty feet in length, by a hundred and fifty in width. Within the enclosure are three large court-yards, each of which is planted with trees and furnished with benches, and contains a wash-house. The first and second courts are divided from one another by a large building containing, on the ground-floor, the workshops of the prisoners, and on the upper floors the cells which form their dormitories. Between the second and third court is the chapel of the inmates which connects the old portion of the building with the infirmary of the second section. A road skirts the walls of the house, so that vehicles may pass to and fro for supplying the needs of the establishment. A wall, from fifteen to eighteen feet in height, encloses the premises.

Two sentinels are on watch night and day, to guard the approaches to the garden, which is situated between the building and the wall of the enclosure. The garden is one hundred and fifteen feet long by sixty feet in width.

To the right of the road may be seen the prison bakery. I visited it, and tasted the brown bread given to the prisoners, and found it good. Each inmate has a right to call for seven hundred grammes, or nearly twenty-five ounces of bread, per day. The bread used for the sick and their attendants is whiter than the ordinary bread.

Almost opposite the bakery stands the kitchen. It is a very large room, and kept in the neatest manner. Five bright copper boilers stand upon an immense stove; the two largest will contain, each, about two hundred and seventy gallons of soup. They were preparing three large hampers of potatoes for the evening meal. I examined the meat used to make soup for the sick, and found it of good quality; and the vegetables seemed to be of the most nutritious and wholesome kind. The depots of supply for the Seine prisons are situated to the left of the outer road.

The front portion of the prison, looking out upon the street, is exclusively occupied by the officers and employés, with the exception of the ground-floor, where are rooms used as depositories for the house linen. The principal façade is a hundred and twenty feet long. These different buildings do not all date from the same epoch. Those which surround the first court-yard bear the date of 1681.

The officers of St.-Lazare are: a director, two chaplains, five clerks, two house-physicians, a "brigadier," a "sous-brigadier," and ten "gardiens," or keepers. Nearly nine thousand inmates pass yearly into St.-Lazare; the ordinary number of inmates at any one time ranges from ten to twelve hundred.

The service of this establishment devolves upon fifty-two religious, besides sixty female domestics, and four "commissionnaires," or messengers, for the needs of the inmates. In general, the keepers are old soldiers; they do not penetrate the interior of the establishment. The interior economy of the house devolves entirely upon the sisters. Since the religious of Marie-Joseph have been intrusted with the charge of this prison—that is to say, for the last fifteen years—two inmates only have succeeded in escaping. The first was employed in the nurses' hall, and had been sent into the garden with some empty bottles, when she climbed over the wall and ran off; but at that time the walls were only nine feet high, and have since been raised to eighteen. The second simply walked out through a door-way used by the sisters, and descended the stairs appropriated exclusively to officers of the house.

She wore a little bonnet and a shawl, so that she very nearly resembled a workwoman. She told the sister on duty that she had come in search of work, that already she had been obliged to wait a long time, and that she was going away, but that she would return another day. The religious, suspecting nothing, opened the door and let her out. In the evening it was reported that one of the prisoners had escaped. From that day to this no one has succeeded in evading the vigilance of the sister on duty.

The objects received by the messengers for delivery to the prisoners, on the part of their friends outside, are first examined by a sister, to insure that nothing prejudicial to morals or discipline may obtain entrance. Sometimes the most ingenious devices are found to have been employed for evading the vigilance of the examiners.

This morning one of the messengers delivered a basket filled with all sorts of provisions, among which were nuts, bread, pies, etc., etc. The nuts were examined one by one; two among them appeared lighter than the others, and on opening them each was found to contain a little scrap of paper, on which were written the answers to be given when the time came for trial. The bread was next examined, in which not the least sign of an opening could be discovered; but the sister, being advised to break it open, found it to contain a box, probably introduced into the dough before baking, and cooked with the bread, which was filled with writing-materials—pens, paper, and stamps—also a letter, the style and autography of which are indescribable. In the pie were found drugs, flowers, truffles, and a phial of cologne-water. These objects, being of a contraband character, were of course confiscated, and the inmate for whom they were intended was punished.

THE PRISON ROUTINE.

Marie, do you wish to know how the prisoners pass the day?

In summer they rise at half-past five o'clock, and in the winter at seven, or at daybreak. Each prisoner makes her own bed, but the domestics sweep the cells. As soon as the prisoners are dressed, each repairs to her own workshop. After singing a hymn and reciting short prayers, they commence work, which they continue without interruption until the hour of breakfast. After breakfast they are allowed an hour's recreation. Then they return to their shops, where they work till dinner, after which another hour of recreation succeeds, and then back to their workshops.

The rosary is recited at five o'clock, and at the end of each decade a couplet from a hymn is sung. A sister selects from one of the books in the library some interesting story, which is read aloud twice a day by one of the prisoners, for the benefit of all. At night they say their prayers in the work-rooms, and in winter go to bed at half-past seven, or in summer at eight. Ordinarily they undress in the dark; however, some of the prisoners have candles, but they are obliged to extinguish them at the expiration of ten minutes.

The cells are secured by enormous iron bolts. The sister on duty in the corridor remains there for half an hour after the prisoners have retired to bed. By means of a little opening about eight inches square, a view of the interior of each cell is obtained. When any prisoner fails to observe the strict silence which is prescribed, the sister taps lightly on the door as a caution; if the disorder continues, she makes a white cross on the door with a bit of chalk. The next morning the sister on duty in the corridor does not withdraw the bolts to doors distinguished by this sign. The offender is brought before the superioress; if the infraction is not grave, she is simply reproved, and sent to her workshop.

On the contrary, if the fault proves to be of a serious nature, the culprit is conducted "au rapport," or to the tribunal of St.-Lazare, where the chief of administration presides, assisted by the superioress. The sister on duty at the time the offence was committed states the charges against the prisoner, and the latter is heard in her defence, for no one is punished without a hearing. The chief of administration pronounces sentence, and the punishment is more or less rigorous according to the nature of the fault committed. The offender never calls the sentence in question, and this would seem to prove its entire justice.

The tribunal holds its sessions every morning at nine o'clock. The prisoners stand in great awe of this tribunal, and sometimes refuse to appear before it, in which case the keepers are sent for to conduct them by force. I heard one of the delinquents say to a religious: "Punish me as much as you please, but do not mention my faults to the mother superioress, and do not send me to the tribunal."

The most frequent punishment in St.-Lazare is confinement in a dungeon; in rare cases a strait-jacket is employed.

THE GARDEN OF ST.-LAZARE.

The garden of St.-Lazare is one of the most calm and peaceful spots in Paris. It is a vast lawn, terminating in two enclosed gardens, with climbing vines and hedges of lilac and other shrubbery, interspersed with splendid acacias, sycamores, and fruit-trees, while the narrow stone walks are bordered with thyme, box, and spring flowers; in fact, the flowers of every season are cultivated here—the peony, rose, lily, dahlia, etc.—all of which are destined only to ornament the altars of the Blessed Virgin, which one meets with at every step in the prison. At the extremity of the garden stands an oratory, and in the middle is a reservoir whence water is drawn for the plants.

The prisoners, under the supervision of a sister, have the entire management of the garden, and consider it a favor to be allowed to come hither to work. Here the air is very pure, and the birds seem to sing their sweetest songs; the rays of the sun play through the graceful branches of the trees, and light up the modest flower-beds beneath. The ear catches on one side the faint murmur of voices from the interior of the prison, on the other the distant rumbling of the streets of Paris.

With these exceptions, solitude reigns supreme, and, indeed, delicious hours might be passed here. If it were possible to turn a deaf ear to the heavy tread of the sentinel who keeps guard at the entrance of the garden, the prison would be forgotten; and could the distant sounds be shut out that indicate the vicinity of the capital, Paris itself would not be thought of. Paris and the prison—the one the legitimate consequence of the other! The following lines would seem to sanction the conjecture that André Chénier and Mdlle. Coigny often walked in the garden of St.-Lazare:

"À Mademoiselle de Coigny, Saint-Lazare.

"Blanche et douce colombe, aimable prisonnière,
Quel injuste ennemi te cache à la lumière?
Je t'ai vue aujourd'hui (que le ciel était beau!)
Te promener longtemps sur le bord du ruisseau;
Au hasard, en tous lieux, languissante, muette,
Tournant tes doux regards et tes pas et ta tête.
Caché dans le feuillage, et n'osant l'agiter,
D'un rameau sur un autre à peine osant sauter,
J'avais peur que le vent décelât mon asile.
Tout seul je gémissais, sur moi-même immobile,
De ne pouvoir aller, le ciel était si beau!
Promener avec toi sur le bord du ruisseau.
Car si j'avais osé, sortant de ma retraite,
Près de ta tête amie aller porter ma tête,
Avec toi murmurer et fouler sous mes pas
Le même pré foulé sous tes pieds délicats,
Mes ailes et ma voix auraient frémi de joie,
Et les noirs ennemis, les deux oiseaux de proie,
Ces gardiens envieux qui te suivent toujours,

Auraient connu soudain que tu fais mes amours.
Tous les deux à l'instant, timide prisonnière,
T'auraient, dans ta prison, ravie à la lumière,
Et tu ne viendrais plus, quand le ciel sera beau,
Te promener encor sur le bord du ruisseau."

. . . .

ANDRÉ CHÉNIER.

I know not of what river André Chénier speaks, for there is in no part of the present garden the slightest trace of a river. This is most likely a poetic license. If not, his imagination must have construed the reservoir into a river.

In the garden all seemed like a summer dream. The day was a warm and lovely one, and I seated myself on a bench at the foot of a tree, near the reservoir. The beautiful acacias waved their feathery branches above, almost concealing from view the sombre walls of the prison. A blackbird was whistling in the distance; an ant, at my feet, was laboriously struggling with a burden larger than itself; a fluttering of wings in the lilac-hedge indicated a bickering among the birds, and occasionally one emerged and flew to the top of the reservoir. Here, dipping his little bill into the water, and raising his head with the glistening drops in his half-open beak, he perceives me and flies away. I closed my book and almost ceased to think, giving myself up to the peace and repose of this delightful solitude, this oasis in the midst of suffering.

I do not know how long this reverie might have

lasted, had not the gate been quietly opened for the ingress of some of the prisoners; there were ten of them, each carrying a pail, with which they proceeded to replenish the reservoir from a fountain close at hand. As they passed they saluted me with a sad smile and a slight inclination of the head, and I returned their salutation.

While they were at work, my attention was attracted particularly to one. She wore, like the others, a coarse blue dress and brown bonnet or cap, but so much of her linen as was apparent was evidently of the finest material. The border of her skirt was trimmed with Valenciennes lace; her fine white stockings half revealed the rosy tint of the skin beneath, and covered a darling little foot enclosed in the daintiest of slippers. On looking at her face I beheld a clear complexion, plump cheeks, black hair, and eyes soft in their expression. She passed with a timid air to empty her pail into the basin, and then returned to the fountain.

I had my book raised, pretending to read, and, as she passed me a second time with her burden, contemplated her without raising my head. She stopped at a little distance from where I was seated, and, setting down her pail with an air of fatigue, drew a long breath, and then began to rub with the left hand the deep imprint left in the right by the iron handle of the pail. I noticed that her hands were small and transparently white, with the blue veins clearly perceptible through the skin, and that her rosy fingernails were carefully trimmed. Said I:

"You are tired, are you not?"

"Yes, madame."

"Very well, then; be seated."

"But where, madame?"

"Here, on this bench."

"Will you permit me?"

"Certainly."

She removed her pail from the middle of the walk, and sat down on the farther end of the bench I continued:

"Is it long since you came to St.-Lazare?"

"Eight days."

"Have you still much longer to stay?"

"Fifteen days."

"Are you unhappy here?"

"It would be supportable but for this costume, which is frightful."

"Your costume, certainly, is not elegant."

"Oh, no! madame."

"It is a punishment, perhaps, for being too fond of embroidered toilets. Does not your conscience suggest this to you?"

"But, madame, it is so natural for a woman to love dress."

"You find it so, do you?"

"Indeed I do. Why has Nature created us beautiful if she did not intend we should correspond with this gift in our manner of dress? For myself, I declare frankly there is no greater happiness in this world than to be able to dress well, and in good taste; my life has been passed in inventing fashions and wearing them."

"Why? That you may gain admiration from others?"

To this she replied, ingenuously:

"With some view to the admiration of others, it is true; but first of all that I may admire myself."

"Then it is the living a life of luxury that has brought you to the condition you are in to-day?"

"Well, yes, madame; remotely, perhaps."

"So, from your ingenious capacity of inventing fashions, you have descended to wearing the style peculiar to St.-Lazare?"

At this remark she hung down her head.

"Well, tell me; how did you commence?"

"My family were possessed of but little, and my dresses were made out of old ones, cleaned and made over by myself. I was in despair because I was not able to procure the thousand little trifles which became me so much, and I looked with envy upon the elegant women who passed me in their carriages, or on the magnificent display of rich fabrics in the shop-windows. When I was offered a handsome toilet, I accepted; and the rest followed as a matter of course. At first I felt my condition somewhat improved, but, the descent once begun, I fell still lower, and now I know not how it will all end. Vanity has been the ruin of me, as it has been of many others."

"That is your belief, is it?" said I.

"Without doubt. You see how luxury and extravagance are blended with our manners; and it is not too much to say that Paris runs riot in sumptuous living. What an array of gay toilets, of rich laces—concealing uneasiness, debts, and ruin! In our day all apparent differences in rank, of grades in society, have disappeared; the fortunes of the rich and the poor man seem to be confounded; all dress alike. Go to the Bois de Boulogne, to the races, to the theatres, and what is there to distinguish the honest woman from the one that is not? Nothing. Again, what is there to distinguish a lady of fortune from one in comfortable circumstances only? Still nothing. The unbridled luxury that envelops Paris, and all of France even, will, perhaps, be the cause of ruining the world!"

Looking sternly at the woman, I said:

"This, then, is your opinion?"

"Yes, madame."

"From what source do you gather your knowledge? The women of your acquaintance? the young people whose society you frequent? Do you believe, then, that honest women all continually run to theatres and races? You are in error. This display is always made by the same women, whom idleness, *ennui*, and the love of dissipation, bring perpetually before the eyes of the public. Three-fourths of them are more or less vitiated; the other fourth is composed in part of rich ladies, who are at least more able to pay for their toilets, and of others in moderate circumstances, who impose upon themselves privations of every kind, or perhaps incur debt, in order to satisfy their vanity. This is a grievous error, no doubt; but when will the day come that honest women will see the necessity of coming out from among their sisters, and dressing themselves in tasteful simplicity, that they may not be confounded with those who submit to luxury as a necessity of their sad condition?"

"So you think, madame, that habits of luxury are less general than are supposed?"

"Yes: before criticising honest women, one should know them."

"It is true. I was wrong, and have spoken too freely. Will you pardon me, madame?"

Just then her companions returned; she rose from the bench, took her pail, and went to rejoin them.

Five minutes later the prisoners had returned to their workshops. I was left alone in the garden, but still the words of the young woman sounded in my ears: "This unbridled luxury that envelops Paris, and all of France even, will be the ruin of the world, perhaps!" I defended reputable women, Marie; but are they indeed without reproach? Who knows? Perhaps this girl knew better than I.

THE "FILLES DES COURS."

In crossing a corridor on the ground-floor, I stopped before a half-opened window to look out upon the prisoners known as "les filles des cours," taking their recreation. This is the designation given to those females who are registered (or licensed) by the police authorities, and are sent here for infringing the rules laid down for the conduct of this class on the street. They occupy the second section. Within a few steps of the window, seated on a bench, was one of these females busily engaged in sewing; another comes to join her, and says:

"Ah! Zoé, what brings you back again to St.-Lazare?"

"I was completely out at elbow, you must know—no more money—no more *hôtel garni.* I had carried the remnants of my goods to my aunt" (meaning the Mont-de-Piété), "and had now got to my last gold-piece (*jaunet*). So, said I to myself, you must go to your country-house at St.-Lazare. I made a rumpus, and tried to stir up the police; but for three days they would take no notice of me. I kept telling them that there were no vacant beds (at least, none for me) in my chateau, and, at last, they grabbed me, and here I am. And you, what brought you here?"

"I made a night of it, and Thomas Folichon paid for the champagne even to his last piece of a hundred sous. I drank too much—I staggered, and went zigzag, and, oh! the streets of Paris are so narrow!"

"So you were fool enough, after drinking champagne, to go and walk on the Boulevards?"

"That's so—confound it! I don't know how it was, but I fell asleep, and on waking I recognized my old home, the office of the Conciergerie; there I got a month in prison for one night's frolic on the streets. But why do you break your back working?"

"I have not one sou; and one must have money here to pay for the glass of wine (*gobette*) from the canteen."

"But you will have your fingers pricked like a seamstress; and perhaps people will think you an honest woman."

The two prisoners who were talking in this manner wore the uniform of St.-Lazare—the dress of blue serge, and the little black cap of the section, only the one standing up wore a superb underskirt of red cashmere, trimmed with black velvet, which formed a train below her prisoner's dress; in her ears she wore coral pendants, and her cap was set upon her head in a fanciful manner. This unique toilet was completed by wooden shoes, of the costume of the house. Zoé lay down her work for a moment to inspect her companion.

"They have not taken away your skirt, Sophie? Faith, it is very coquettish, but your shoes are a devilish contrast."

"I wore here loves of shoes; but, when a poor woman was leaving yesterday without any, I told her to take my shoes (*bichons*), and that is the last of them."

"Well, do you like it here?"

"Not much: before, we used to have good times, but now there is no way of amusing one's self. The sisters vex one so; they make us get down upon our knees, and compel us to go to mass; and, even if we do not listen to the sermon, one cannot help hearing a little. Last Sunday I cried like a fool."

"Now, don't go to the convent, like Malaine."

"Well, that's better than to die a *bleue*" (lower even than the filles des cours) "like Fifine."

Upon which the foolish creature left, humming a song. I have given you, dear Marie, some idea of the style of conversation in this section, and I am sure it is as distasteful to you as it is to me.

The greater number of those belonging to this section are young girls, but there are others who are very old. I spoke to a passing domestic, and asked her:

"Why are these old women shut up here?"

She answered:

"Madame, there are several such here, but of different classes. Do you see, yonder, that tall woman, very well appearing, with gray hair?"

"Yes."

"Very well; she is what they call a *procureuse*."

"What, pray, is a *procureuse?*"

"It is a woman who plays the part of a great lady; introducing herself into poor families where interesting young girls may be found; giving aid to the parents and articles of dress to the daughter, and then passing herself off as a generous protectress, or even a lady patroness, but always as a rich woman. She assumes the exterior of respectability, and, in fact, can play any *rôle*. She is unceasing in her attentions until the time comes for her to fulfil her commission for the old debauchee into whose hands she finally places her prize. The authorities watch these characters well, and when detected they are severely punished; but sometimes they manage to escape notice."

I think, Marie, that all charitable ladies should be furnished with letters from the priest of their parish before going to visit a poor family for the first time. If every one were to go fortified in this manner, the procuress would not be able to pass herself off as a patroness.

[The author goes on to describe two other classes of bad women to be found in this section—the *coqueuses* and the *marcheuses*—in regard to whom it would be discreet to omit particulars.]

How sad this all is! Fathers and mothers of families little suspect the dangers their children run in this wicked capital.

Whenever a "fille des cours" grossly violates the police code which regulates her class, she is arrested and taken to the office of the Conciergerie. Here the Sisters of Marie-Joseph have been lately introduced to receive such prisoners. The following day the girl is taken to St.-Lazare. The carriage used for this purpose is a kind of omnibus, painted black and yellow. On their arrival here the prisoners' names are entered on the register, and they are searched in the "Vestiaire." They are very desirous of retaining their jewels, and, in order to do so, often conceal them in their stockings, or in the tucks of their dresses, so that they may not be taken from them.

The first night, they sleep in a large hall, situated on the ground-floor, just beside the shops. This hall contains about twenty or thirty beds. They are carefully guarded, and generally sleep in the clothing they wore on entering; at least, no bed-clothing is provided here.

The next day, after undergoing inspection by the doctors, some are sent to the infirmary and others to the workshops, first changing their dress for the costume of the prison. The inmates of the first section (the *détenues*) are not subjected to this change of costume, but continue to wear their own clothing until after trial or conviction. When they enter the house, they are also immediately assigned their cells, instead of passing a night in the hall before mentioned. The filles des cours are not disorderly in St.-Lazare; generally they are quiet and docile. I overheard two of them talking, and one says to the other:

"My dear, I believe there is a Supreme Being."

"Why do you make that reflection?"

"Because, when we are on the streets, it takes sometimes two or three sergents de ville to arrest us, but at St.-Lazare one little sister is sufficient to march us in battalion order."

The other replied:

"You are right; there must be a Supreme Being."

THE "FILLE DE JOIE."

A STORM arose suddenly while I was in the chapel. It was three o'clock in the afternoon, and when I desired to return to my room it was raining in torrents; the outside road was inundated and in no condition to use; the interior corridors were crowded by the "filles des cours," who at that time were taking their recreation. I had not the courage to go that way and encounter them, and in order to pass the time I entered into conversation with the sister on guard before the entrance to their hall, and we took turns at looking through the little opening that gave a view of the long corridors.

There were present fully three hundred prisoners, and a cloud of smoke floated over their heads. I spied in the angle of a window a young woman, small, thin, and pale, smoking a cigarette; the sister on service within the corridor advanced toward her; the latter perceived her and concealed her cigarette, lighted as it was, in the pocket of her apron, and joined a group near by. I had a full view of her face; her great black eyes, lighting up her pale visage, gave her an air of wonderful energy; she spoke with vehemence, and laughed loudly, but, when the sister had gone away, she again took out her cigarette, returned to her former place, and commenced smoking anew. I said to the religious:

"What is the name of that pale girl near the window, who smokes so vigorously?"

She looked through the little door, and replied:

"It is Euphrasie—a singular creature; not ungovernable, but whimsical and capricious; sometimes overcome with sadness, sometimes turbulently gay."

"You appear to know her well?"

"Yes; she is an *habituée* of St.-Lazare."

"I should like to see her nearer."

The sister opened the door which separated us from the inmates, and made a sign to one of them, who came toward us.

"I want to see Euphrasie," said she.

Euphrasie threw away her cigarette and approached. The sister said to her:

"Euphrasie, will you talk a little with the lady?"

"I don't care if I do."

I led her into the sacristy, and seated myself at an oak table before the window. Euphrasie took a stool a few steps from me.

"My child, how old are you?"

"Twenty-two years."

"And you are an inmate here?"

"Yes."

"Have you been here often?"

"Oh, yes! I began my course early."

"Are you happy?"

At this she arose quickly and proceeded to the door.

"You are curious, madame; you wish to know too much."

I stopped her.

"Now, Euphrasie, do not go yet."

She returned, and, surveying me from head to foot, said:

"After all, what is it to you whether we are happy or unhappy? You are not a woman of our kind; do not concern yourself about us."

I made a sign for her to sit down, and said:

"Who was the means of bringing you to this condition?"

A flash of anger lit up her eyes as she replied:

"My father. I was thirteen years old, and at fourteen I had already left my mother."

She seated herself: an agonized expression passed over her features.

"If you could know, madame, the miseries, the privations, of that wretched life—the days without food, the nights without shelter, the ill-treatment, the insults, the contempt I have endured, and the dangers that I have run!"

"The dangers? What kind of dangers?"

"I have been on the point, several times, of meeting a violent death. One day I had been drinking, for I drank, madame, as almost all the girls of my profession do. I accidentally went into a basement wine-shop; men, half-drunk, were seated around a long, dirty table, covered with cards and empty bottles. I seated myself among them; they offered me liquor, and I drank again. The smoke of the gas and of their pipes, and the alcohol I drank, made me completely tipsy. It was eleven o'clock at night. The master of the house came to close up his shop, when a man sleeping upon the corner of a table woke and recognized me. 'Look,' said he to his comrades, 'here is Euphrasie, the courtezan; a fine lot, upon my word.' 'She is a fille de joie,' replied another; 'then she belongs to us; what shall we do with her?' Whereupon they all rose up, made a circle around me, and deliberated upon what disposition to make of me. Little by little their hideous, besotted faces became ferocious; one of them, solemnly extending his hand, said, 'Let us hang her.'

"These words suddenly brought me to my senses, and, comprehending the whole danger of my position, a shudder ran through me. I had some money upon my person; making an excuse to stoop down, I slipped it in my shoes. As I raised my eyes I saw that they had all taken off their cravats, and were tying them together to make a halter. 'Where shall we hang her?' said one of them. 'To the gas-pipe,' said another, 'we can see her better there.' I screamed; the master of the house ran in; there was a quarrel—a scuffle; I was struck; and the bottles began to fly around.

"I was wounded in the head; the sight of my blood flowing increased their fury. 'We must finish her,' vociferated another. 'Yes; at least, unless the girl pays her ransom.' 'I have gold; I will pay for drink for you!' exclaimed I. 'Gold! gold!' shrieked the men. They searched me, but found nothing. 'If you will spare my life you shall have gold,' I repeated. 'She lies; she has none. Let us hang her!' I took off my shoes, and hastily drew forth several louis d'or.

"At this their drunken eyes brightened up, and they rushed upon me, snatched it away, and began to drink again. The proprietor of the shop profited by this diversion to open a little door, and thrust me outside. I was safe, and at liberty; but the wind and cold of the night penetrated me. I staggered along for some minutes, and then crouched in the corner of a carriage-way, and fell into a stupor.

"At the break of day I came to myself; my clothing was besmeared with mud, and stained with wine; I was in great suffering, and, when I recalled the events of the past night, I hated myself. I resolved to put an end to my life, and slowly made my way toward the Seine. The rays of the rising sun shone upon the river; a tree upon the road beside it swayed its green branches in the morning wind; the sky was clear, and silence reigned around, for the city was still asleep. I seated myself on the bank; only a step separated me from the stream, and I paused to think.

"I looked back upon my infancy, the miserable life I had led, my present situation; and, putting all together, my disgust for life returned with redoubled force. I saw myself disgraced, humbled, despised; I wondered how the sun could bless me with its light, or the winds salute me with their breath; I shed tears of agony; my feelings became too desperate for resistance; I arose, and with one bound precipitated myself into the Seine. The waters whirled and eddied as they carried me down; I remembered no more."

Euphrasie, on finishing her recital, glided from the stool to the floor and sat there, her eyes fixed and motionless, and her lips parted with an expression of horror; she seemed overwhelmed with her feelings. "And this," said I to myself, regarding her with amazement, "this is one whom society, with dreadful irony, calls a 'fille de joie.'" Words failed me, and silent tears flowed from my eyes. Euphrasie, recalled to herself, looked at me.

"You weep, madame."

"Yes."

"And why?"

"I weep for you."

She reseated herself upon the stool, and continued:

"Happy would it have been for me if I had died—but I did not. A dog came to my rescue, and held me up to the surface; I was picked up and put into a boat, and a sergent de ville brought me to the police office. I was a *fille isolée* then, but I have borne a heavier burden since."

"Are the *filles isolées* more free, then?"

"Not much more, madame; they cannot go out when they please, nor can they go *where* they please. A girl of our class is a prisoner in Paris. The boulevards, the public squares, the promenades, and the quays, are forbidden us; the Champs Elysées, with their gardens and beautiful trees, we are not allowed to enter. I have been arrested at least ten times in the Champs Elysées. Sometimes the temptation proved too much for me; when I have not seen the green grass for a long time, nothing can restrain me from sitting for an hour or two in the shade, and for this I get a month in St.-Lazare."

Meanwhile the storm continued, the wind blew in gusts, the rain beat against the window-panes; it thundered heavily, and a flash of lightning illuminated the sacristy. Euphrasie trembled, made the sign of the cross, and bowed her head.

"Madame, it is terrible to hear the thunder, but it is beautiful, it is grand!"

She drew from the pocket of her dress a little bag of tobacco and some paper, and busied herself with making a cigarette. She appeared to have forgotten the storm, the thunder, and even my presence.

"Euphrasie," said I, "why do you smoke?"

She adroitly slipped her finished cigarette into her sleeve.

"Pardon me, madame, I forgot. I smoke, that is a fact; to smoke is my greatest happiness. In the houses where we live, we are not permitted to go out but once in fifteen days; it is a great while to be without seeing the sun. When I get tired of my confinement, I seat myself upon the floor, or upon a cushion, and smoke all day long; then I have waking dreams; I seem to see the country, the hills, the green grass, and, above all, the pure, limpid, blue lake. I was not made for the life that I lead; when I think too much, despair turns my brain; then I drink, sing, do every thing to forget myself; if I did not do this, I should kill myself."

"Euphrasie, you must not think of dying; think of living as an honest woman."

"Your advice, madame, is very good. There is no woman who does not wish to be so; it is such a fine thing to be an honest women. Ah! if they themselves only knew their own value! I have sometimes shed bitter tears, when, through a half-opened window (for the glass in ours is roughened, and we cannot see through it into the street), I have seen an honorable woman saluted on the street as she passed."

"Then try to become one yourself."

"I should like to, but I cannot. Our lives are passed in dissipation. We go into a house, we drink, we dine, and lead a gay life; one month after we have neither money nor clothes; every thing belongs to the mistress of the house, of whom we hire our dresses. We are in debt, and sometimes we are slaves as long as we live."

"What a shame!"

"I think there is nothing in society that is more disgraceful."

The sister now came to give us notice that the hour of recreation was over. I drew from my pocket a rosary, and wound it around the arm of Euphrasie, saying:

"Promise me that you will keep this, and that you will sometimes recite it; perhaps God will draw you out of this abyss."

"I will, madame; thank you. I shall always remember that you have shed tears of pity over a poor *fille de joie.*"

Then she slowly withdrew.

I felt my heart bursting with inexpressible agony; I turned again toward the entrance, and looked through the little grated opening. Euphrasie was running from one group to another; never had she been more gay; her laughter was heard above all the voices in the hall. The sister said to me:

"I cannot comprehend why Euphrasie leaves you in so gay a humor."

"I understand," returned I; "she wishes to forget, but I shall not forget her."

Ten minutes later all the "girls of the street" were at work in their shops, and silence reigned through the long corridors they had just quitted.

I experienced a sort of dread in traversing them; the atmosphere suffocated me, and I hastened to an open door that I might breathe the fresh air. The rain had ceased, some light clouds passed rapidly across the sky, and the blue heavens reappeared; the birds were sporting among the dripping branches of the trees, and shaking the moisture from their wings. The storm had passed from the sky, but the tempest of my heart was not quieted, Marie.

To what a frightful study I have condemned myself for your sake! How I suffer! I had a fever that night, and all the "filles de joie" seemed to be invading my chamber, and delivering themselves up to mad revelry. A shower of gold rained around them, and fell with a hollow sound into the mud that they were piling up around me. Suddenly one of the girls from the infirmary, pale and attenuated, appeared at my door; she advanced slowly and gained my bedside. In spite of the desperate efforts I made, I could not repel her nor escape her icy touch. In short, I suffered the most dreadful nightmare I ever experienced in my life. O Marie, how terrible a thing is vice! What defilement does it not leave in its train!

August 10th.

Dear Marie, the condition of woman is at present creating great interest in the minds of the reflecting portion of society. If God had placed me in an influential position, through fortune, rank, or talents, I would have been willing to consecrate my life to the amelioration of my sex, but, in the modest sphere to which I am limited, I can do nothing. At the same time the character of woman has been my life-long study. My opportunities for observing women in every class of society have been extraordinary.

You know I lived a long time in the country, where I was able to examine at my leisure the life of the peasantry in their frugal homesteads. In the city I have carefully studied the life of the working-women, as also the life of women in the middle classes, and finally of those of the higher classes. There was one class that I could not know at all, and that I had never tried to know—the class of fallen women. The thought of their very existence was dreadful to me. When but the words "lost woman" were pronounced in my hearing, I hung my head in confusion, as if the shame of a portion must fall upon the whole sex. I asked myself often, do they still merit the name of women? I answered, no; they have become I know not what; of whom Bossuet says, "They have not a name in any language."

Very well, dear friend, Providence took me by the hand and led me into St.-Lazare! And, when I saw myself in the presence of vice, I experienced a feeling of repulsion I cannot describe; I revolted at the thought of breathing the same air with the guilty ones. Even in looking upon them from a distance I trembled; for several days I contended against my feelings, but without being able to overcome my disgust.

One day the superior said laughingly to me:

"Decidedly you are afraid of the inmates; you must see them near, once, and all that feeling will pass away."

She took my arm in hers, and we visited all the halls, all the shops, and all the infirmaries. At first I saw nothing, so greatly was I agitated. The inmates saluted us, I returned the salutation; then, when I presumed to look upon them, little by little my curiosity resumed sway. I studied them. After my return from this lengthened inspection of every species of misery, degradation, and suffering, my fears gave place to excessive pity. I may say, Marie, that I have now come to know all classes and conditions of the female sex, and I do not hesitate to declare that the happiest condition of all, in my view, is that of the country-woman.

If the peasant-women only knew the advantages their humble position possesses, would they ever consent to leave their country-homes and come to live in a crowded city? You know as well as I that a cottage in the country is far preferable to the ante-chambers or kitchens of Paris. These pretty cabins, with their tiled roofs, are the abodes of peace. How many times I have rested under these calm and rustic roofs! On my approach the dog barks to give notice; on recognizing me, the children come running out to meet me, the dog ceases to bark, while the mother of the family makes haste to finish feeding her chickens, in order to prepare for me the best chair her humble cot affords.

Sometimes it is the hour for the family meal; on a bare table is arranged the great brown earthen platter, filled with smoking vegetables. What appetites have the cottagers! How savory is the bread of this little quiet home after the labors of the day! While the good man eats his dinner, the busy housewife arranges and commands; here she is in her element. She chases out the chicken that has the boldness to enter to take part in the repast by picking up the crumbs that fall from the table, or caresses the dog who is smelling the bread in the child's hands.

Only to think that a young girl of sixteen should so early become dissatisfied with her cottage-home, and turn her face toward the city, where bright ribbons and crosses of gold dazzle her sight!

Now let us trace the history of this little peasant-girl. In this humble, whitewashed cabin, encircled by creeping vines, she was born. Her mother nourished her at her own bosom, and guided her first steps over the greensward which surrounds their homestead. The favorite companion of her plays was this dog, the faithful guardian of her humble home. At six years of age she already assists her mother in the labors of the house; she carries the bundle of grass to the white goat which has so often supplied her with sustenance. At ten years she superintends the family meals, and goes into the forests in search of dry wood to replenish the fire on the modest hearth. At twelve, after being prepared by the pious village pastor, she makes her first communion.

Then commences her life of real labor. She weeds the garden, gathers together the vegetables already dug up, and begins to earn her daily bread. At fifteen comes the season of youthful pleasures, and she takes part in the gay dances of her female companions, who meet together every Sunday during the beautiful summer months; or during the long winter evenings, seated by the cheerful fire, she listens to the recital of some fearful or amusing story. This happy period continues, until one day, at a turn in a path bordered with hawthorn, a young man of the village, whom she has several times avoided meeting, directly encounters her, and, resolutely intercepting her, says:

"I wish to be married; will you be my wife?"

She is betrothed. The conjugal nest is prepared. At the time fixed upon she becomes a happy and chaste spouse. Children come, one after the other, to enliven their humble home; she caresses them, brings them up, and establishes them in life. Finally, she settles into a peaceful old age. It is true that in this calm life there are some stormy days, and there are inclement seasons, when hail destroys the harvests. Even so; but where is there a life without suffering, especially for a woman? I know of no exceptions.

Is the female of the laboring class in cities as happy? I think not. Her birthplace is an attic. There the summer heats are suffocating, the cold of winter is intense. Life is supported with difficulty; the bread with which the child is supplied is earned by the sweat of the mother's brow, and has often to be even measured out. At twelve the child is already wearily at work in the shop at which she is apprenticed. At sixteen she is a finished workwoman, and labors all day, and sometimes a part of the night, to procure the mere necessaries of life. Her business almost always brings her in contact with the rich and the well-to-do, the contrast making her feel her own poverty all the more keenly. She next becomes a wife and mother. The salary of her husband is insufficient to give bread to her children, Together with the cares of maternity and those of the household, she is subject to the unceasing demands of labor. What has she not to suffer should sickness, want of work, or the misconduct of her husband, bring misery to their garret?

The women of the middle classes ordinarily enjoy the period of youth. It is true that they are for the most part obliged to submit, at that time of life, to the captivity of the convent or the boarding-school, where they have long lessons, and are obliged to study, and must, besides, be separated from their mothers and be cut off from their homes. The peasant and the work-women at least keep their children with them; the well-to-do mother believes it her duty to confide her daughter to the hands of strangers.

This is a terrible evil, the most pernicious error of our time; an error that brings about the unhappiness of the greater part of our young girls. In establishments for public instruction children forget all family ties, they learn nothing of interior management, of house-keeping, and adapt themselves to no regular pursuit in life. When they leave the boarding-school, their knowledge is limited to a little orthography and a superficial idea of history. They play the piano tolerably, but nothing is known thoroughly, and consequently no useful result is obtained.

If the young person is rich, or has fortune sufficient to invite a husband, she will make but an indifferent mistress of a house. If she has no marriage portion she will not marry at all, that is certain, and her position is a sad one. As she has no establishment, she is without resources for the future. So long as she is young, gay, and fond of amusement, she will enliven the house of her parents, and at first all will go well.

But the time will come when she will perceive that she is destined to become an old maid. Her parents will also, as years advance, look upon her as a burden. Then embarrassments will arise, and some day the father will signify to his daughter that she must earn her own living; this intimation will fill her heart with sadness and bitterness. If, by chance, she be a person of intelligence and energy, she will become an assistant teacher, lady's companion, or clerk in a store. If neither of these occupations is suited to her capacity, what will become of her? It is impossible to say; perhaps her destiny will be to pass through St.-Lazare: I have seen such cases here.

Do not tell me that I exaggerate, Marie, for what I say is too true. Nor should you accuse me of being too severe upon the father of the family. No; I do not blame him for his course; it is natural. See the animals; they nurse their young, they find a shelter for them, and defend them from harm; but when they have matured, even the mother refuses to recognize them any longer.

When I was a child I had a white cat that I loved very much, because she showed so much affection for her little ones. When her kittens were too numerous it was necessary to use every imaginable precaution in taking any from her, and after doing so we had to hear her mournful cries for two or three days. She never quitted the two that were left her, night or day, and we were even obliged to carry her food to her; she licked her little kittens, caressed them, and carried them by the neck into the open air, and, when they first commenced to eat, she would not touch the milk-soup that was prepared for them. Could devotion be greater? Very well, when these little kittens were old enough to dispense with the care of a mother she neglected them; and when they were well grown she would not even look at them; she boxed them, and bit them, and battled with them to such a degree, that, to restore peace, we were obliged to give the young ones away.

Do not allege, my friend, that this isolated fact signifies nothing; it signifies much, because the lesson is repeated throughout Nature.

Do not reproach me, either, for comparing man with the animals. Man is very superior to them, no doubt: he is possessed of reason, and this is why he sometimes supports his children as long as he lives; it is no longer the paternal instinct which guides him in this, it is duty and reason.

I contend that it is necessary to change the system of education for girls of the middle classes, that is, for the daughters of merchants, of artists, of civil officers, of physicians, and even of nobles of small means; for all such, in fact, as are to receive an ordinary education and no more. As to young ladies belonging to the higher classes, I wish to say but little, because they form the exception, and I only pretend to study the masses. It is necessary, no doubt, that a princess should be educated for her own particular sphere. At the same time, would it not be better to cast a glance into the future, in order to be prepared for reverses of fortune? In this age of social changes, there is no one that can say to himself, "I am perfectly secure from misfortune." Sovereigns have been seen giving lessons in mathematics, and noble ladies making shoes as a means of living in a strange land. I am persuaded in my own mind that every woman ought to be brought up to some special calling.

Allow me, Marie, to draw my conclusions. The condition of the peasant-woman is the happiest, because she possesses in abundance all the essentials of comfort; she should be persuaded to remain in the country, and to continue in that state of life. The work-woman labors much and earns but little; work that will prove the most remunerative should be found for her, so that her life may be a less painful one. The girls of the middle classes receive inadequate education; incomplete, in that it does not secure to them resources for the future. Firstly, they should be brought up at home; secondly, they should be given a position.

August 12th.

It is a great creation, that of woman; I never more fully comprehended this truth than yesterday. I was seated in the chapel, in meditation before the statue of the Blessed Virgin; I said to myself: "Christianity has not only regenerated woman, but has also revealed to us her true greatness. Catholicism has admirably symbolized her in the Virgin Mother, whom she has placed upon her altars. She is a virgin, that is to say, all that is beautiful and pure in Nature; something uncontaminated by man, and unsullied by his touch; an atmosphere that is not tainted by the impure, the brilliant azure of the firmament unobscured by clouds; the sweet perfume of flowers that no human being has drunk in; the delicate velvet of ripe fruit that has never lost its freshness by contact.

"She is a mother, that is to say, perfection in the moral order, hers is the power that gives life, the tenderness that sweetens it, the devotion that sustains it, and the memory which endures long after the life of the loved one is swallowed up in death. She is a mother who ceases not to be a virgin; and is thus an ideal of the infinite. As a woman, she is without stain, even in her maternity; great by her conformity to the Divine will, her greatness is not lessened through the child given to her womb, and whom she nourishes at her own breast. She retains the grace of virginity, while she wields the power of a mother. Such is the woman, as Christianity sets her before us in the person of her whom all generations shall call blessed. Such is woman as I comprehend her."

And now, Marie, what has man made of this chosen creature? During long centuries of barbarism, he has caused her to bend under a disgraceful slavery, rendering her, in fact, the slave of slaves, wounding her delicate members by confinement in hateful bonds, exhausting her strength by burdens too heavy for her weakness to endure.

Do you believe her situation better to-day, because man flatters while he ruins her? Ah! that you could be witness, as I am, to the tears, the nights of sleeplessness, the despair of the unhappy one who has been led astray from the path of rectitude, her nature perverted, her honor sacrificed, a suffering, abandoned, despised creature, who has nothing to expect in the future but misery and shame! Why? Because she has given her heart, and surrendered her virtue to a wretch. When once the breath of impurity has tarnished her soul, she is changed from her former self, her evil instincts are developed, guilty thoughts take possession of her mind, and vice reigns in her heart. She exclaims, like the reprobate represented in Scripture, "Let us eat and drink, for to-morrow we die."

She revels in the basest criminality, rushes madly into bacchanalian orgies, until, at twenty years of age, pale, disfigured, and worn out, she seeks the bed of a hospital. To her, there is no more any thing lovely or pure in creation; her breath vitiates the air; her hand withers the flowers, her appearance even is frightful to the pure woman. No refuge exists but one, the mercy of God, ever lending hope to the penitent. Oh, how often I have seen them weep in presence of the sanctuary! I have trembled with fear, and my heart has been moved to deepest pity at the spectacle. Marie, if God had given me eloquence, I would cry aloud to all my sex: "O woman, avoid the declivity that conducts to these fatal paths; from the moment the first evil step is taken, you will rapidly descend to the depths of the abyss! The poisoned cup is wreathed with flowers, the descent is decorated with foliage, as green shrubbery is placed around tombs, to veil the corruption within." But, ah! my voice is weak and impotent, and will not be heeded, and it is left to me alone to profit by the dreadful lesson before me.

August 13th.

The sky is so blue this morning, dear Marie, that it seems to me I once more look upon the sky of our own Provence, the sun shines brilliantly and the air is soft; my joyous little swallows describe large circles in their flight, and then return, with hasty curve of the wing, to their little ones. The prisoners are taking their recreation; they appear to me gayer than usual. The imagination of woman is so susceptible, one ray of the sun is sufficient to make her forget her suffering! God has been good to her in giving her the faculty of forgetting quickly, for her destiny is (happy as she may sometimes appear to be) to suffer much.

THE REFECTORY.

I HAVE paid a visit to the Refectory, without doubt the most beautiful hall in St.-Lazare. It is the same that the Lazarist fathers used before the Revolution, and affords space for nearly two hundred persons at table. The entablature of the door is richly sculptured, and under the present administration a tesselated floor has been laid. The refectory is on the ground-floor, and has on the right ten windows, overlooking the road around the house, and six openings on the second court. Twelve long, unpainted tables, placed in three rows, and surrounded by benches, form the furniture of the room. Nine pillars running down in the centre of the hall support the ceiling. Two large stoves warm this vast room. A crucifix, with a Christ of the size of life, is suspended upon the wall above the estrade, or small raised platform, occupied by the sister whose duty it is to preside here. She recites the *Benedicite* * in a loud voice, and silence reigns during the meal.

The domestics were setting the table when I entered. Each prisoner has a porringer with tinned-iron spoon, etc. Some metal cups, and a pitcher of

* The first word of the *grace* said at meals in a religious house.

the same material, are placed in the centre of the table. 'The pitcher contains water, the ordinary drink of the inmates; but if they prefer a glass of wine they can procure it by paying fifteen centimes, or one cent and a half, and this is what is called a *gobette*. The prisoners bring their own bread to table, it being distributed to them every morning in the workshops.

They take two meals a day, and go to the refectory by divisions; breakfast is served from eight o'clock to ten, and dinner from two to four. In the morning, they have vegetable soup, and on Thursdays and Sundays meat-soup. Their fare at dinner is invariably as follows: On Sundays, beef and dried peas; Monday, red beans; Tuesday, rice; Wednesday, potatoes; Thursday, beef and pulse; Friday, white-beans; Saturday, potatoes. The vegetables are cooked in fat. The prisoners rarely finish their meals in the refectory; almost all are supplied with a brown-earthen porringer, and they carry their food with them into the court-yard, and terminate the meal during the time of recreation.

August 15th.

I have taken a particular fancy, my dear, to one of the young prisoners. I met with her in the infirmary of the first section. She was seated upon her bed, and her flaxen hair floated around her pretty face, giving it a sweet but sad expression. I asked her name. She told me it was Valentine.

She appears very timid; every time I spoke to her, she blushed, then grew pale, then wept; however, I never passed through the room without saluting her. Yesterday, as I was leaving her, she raised my hand to her lips and kissed it. It occurred to me, for the first time, to inquire of the sister the cause of her detention, for I could not imagine what misconduct this frail, sweet creature could be guilty of. The sister replied:

"She is a criminal, madame; she is accused of infanticide."

I was thunderstruck.

"How, this young girl a mother, and the murderess of her child?"

"Yes, madame."

I was deeply saddened at this information. I asked myself how it was possible for such a creature to be so cruel. I approached the bed.

"Valentine," said I, "I know that you are good, and I love you, but you have suffered much; you will tell me your history, will you not?"

She bowed her flaxen head in her hands, and replied:

"Never, madame, I could not. You would despise me, perhaps, and abandon me, and your kindness has done me so much good."

"Despise you, my child? Do not believe it. I wish only that your unhappiness may prove a warning to others. You promise me, do you not?"

She looked at me through her tears.

"If you wish, madame, I will take courage to relate to you my sad history."

"I will return to-morrow, and you will tell me all."

"Yes, madame."

I left her, but was tormented all day by the thought, How at her age could one have thus lost sight of the duty of a woman, and a mother? Her history will reveal all.

To-day I went to pay my promised visit to Valentine. She turned very pale on seeing me. Her bed is placed in a corner of the room, and the neighboring beds were empty. The sick who were able to walk were grouped together at the extremity of the room, and we were alone. I seated myself beside her cot upon a stool, and took one of her hands in mine, saying to her:

"My poor child, I am ready to hear what you have to say."

She answered me sadly:

"You alone shall know the whole truth, madame; to tell you it shall be my expiation."

I sat silent, and she began.

THE INFANTICIDE.

"I WAS born in a little village in Normandy. My father was a landholder who owned a good property, lived happily, and was held in esteem by his neighbors. I was his only child, and, until I was seven years of age, I lived at home. My mother loved me with a blind affection, and shed bitter tears when it became necessary for us to part; for the vanity of my father induced him to send me to the best boarding-school in the neighboring village, so that I might be made a lady of.

"In this school I remained until I was fifteen. I was quick, and learned rapidly, so that, when I returned home, my parents found their fondest expectations realized. My father's establishment now struck me as being very contracted, and his manners as unpolished, but, as my heart was not bad, and my judgment was upright, I endeavored to adapt myself to my circumstances.

"I suffered, however, for a taste had been cultivated in me for elegances; the arts and literature attracted me, the manners of elegant people captivated me. I concealed my unhappiness, but I created an ideal world, and lived in that.

"I had been betrothed, at an early age, to the

son of one of my father's friends, and, although there was nothing in him to awaken my enthusiasm, I was habituated to the thought of becoming his wife.

"Andrew, for such was his name, was good, simple, and very affectionate. I had a strong friendship for him, but no love. That calm sentiment satisfied me, because I knew no other.

"To relieve the solitude I experienced, when my domestic occupations were over for the day, I was accustomed to take long and solitary walks in the fields, or on the sea-shore. I sought out the paths which wound over the banks; these were always carpeted with green, and, when the sun began to decline, I would seat myself upon a moss-covered cliff, look out upon the ocean, and watch the changing of the sombre waters, as wave rolled after wave, and gleams of light shot forth, and then disappeared. I watched the tide, as it rose silently, gaining little by little on the sandy beach, until it broke upon the pebbles beyond, and rolled them to and fro with a hollow sound.

"Then, my soul was stirred with new emotions: the breeze from the ocean, the last rays of the sun, burying themselves in the waves, the monotonous plaints of the sea, all excited my imagination. I was moved and troubled, for I felt myself alone, with no one to admire with me the beauties of Nature. Disquieted and agitated, I longed for a soul to sympathize with mine.

"Then, I quitted the shore for the fields, and even here I was sad. Repose reigned everywhere;

the cows were chewing at their ease the salt grass; from the village arose the sound of the children's voices at their play; the smoke peacefully curled above the chimneys of the cottages, giving sign of the evening meal in preparation. All was calm: I alone was not at rest. I bowed my head in my hands, and wept bitterly.

"On a little elevation near the village was a large wooden cross, supported by two or three rustic stone steps. Ordinarily, before returning home, I repaired thither to kneel and pray; there, peace overspread my soul, as the dew descends from heaven; I then dried my tears, arose, and proceeded homeward. I embraced my mother, welcomed my betrothed, and forgot the storm that had passed over my soul. Still, the day after saw it renewed.

"One evening, when I had been more than usually agitated, I quitted the sea-shore with hasty steps, without noticing the beautiful flowers which enamelled the sward, and which I thoughtlessly crushed. As I proceeded, I found myself near the cross, and a few steps more would have brought me to it, when, raising my eyes, I perceived a stranger standing upon the lower step. He was young and richly attired; his black hair floated around his high forehead, which was as white as a woman's, and a delicate mustache adorned his lip. I had ample leisure to notice him, for he was standing motionless, absorbed in the contemplation of the sea.

"I was fascinated. Never before had I beheld one of so aristocratic a bearing. In appearance he surpassed the ideal of my dreams. I felt glued to the spot, and dared not attempt to move. The stranger, however, soon perceived me; he advanced toward me, saluting me with the most exquisite courtesy, and asked me for some information about the locality. I replied tremblingly: I felt awkward and embarrassed; and as soon as possible made my way, like a frightened bird, to the village.

"At the foot of the hill I stopped to take breath, for my heart beat as if I should suffocate.

"Overwhelmed with surprise at my emotion, I resumed my path, but, before losing sight of the eminence I had quitted, an irresistible impulse led me to look back; the stranger was still standing where I had seen him, but he was no longer looking toward the ocean; his gaze was riveted on me. When he perceived me turn toward him, he saluted me again. I then comprehended in an instant my imprudence, but it occasioned me no regret. It already seemed to me that a mysterious tie united me to the unknown; a rush of joy dilated every fibre of my heart; every thing grew bright before me.

"I passed a sleepless night; but, when morning dawned, a reaction passed over me. I reflected on what had occurred, and was agitated with fear. Why should this stranger have so attracted me? I knew him not, and perhaps should never meet him again. Ought I indeed even desire to?

"Profound sadness now filled my soul, the sun seemed obscured, and the earth joyless; after giving way to a flood of tears, I sincerely resolved not to return to the spot, for fear that I should again meet the stranger. All day long, I remained in a state of depression.

"At a short distance from the village, in an opposite direction from the beach, stood a small oratory, dedicated to the Blessed Virgin, which had been erected ages ago by a huntsman, who had lost his way during a storm, and came near perishing by being precipitated into a ravine. This oratory was open day and night, and, for more than nine hundred years, had afforded shelter to persons overtaken by storms. The young girls of the village came there to deposit at the feet of the Mother of God either a garland of corn-flowers or a bouquet of Marguerites gathered in the fields; while the laborers, as they passed by it, respectfully uncovered their heads. I directed my steps toward this oratory, hoping to appease the turmoil in my heart by praying to Mary.

"As I stepped upon the threshold, the stranger was before me! He dipped his finger in the holy-water font at the door, and courteously held it toward me. I drew back, but, overcome by emotion, leaned for support against the wall outside. Perceiving my agitation, he came forth, and, placing my arm in his, led me to a grassy knoll, where he caused me to sit down until I should recover myself. Placing himself meanwhile at my feet, he addressed me in a sweet, caressing tone, as though he were comforting and reassuring a child.

"Although he spoke to me for a long time, I was too much agitated to understand all he said, and only noted the exquisite harmony of his voice. Little by little I took courage to look at him. His dark-blue eyes beamed with a light that penetrated to the bottom of my heart. I endeavored to struggle against the influences I felt myself under, and fly—but in vain; an invisible bond held me to the individual before me. I felt that my existence belonged to this man, who had been a stranger to me until the evening before.

"On leaving me, he made me promise that I would see him again the next day. The Vicomte Maximin de —— had come to visit a watering-place in the adjoining village, and was making an excursion to ours, when he met me. This is the man who was the cause of my misfortunes.

"He returned every day, and we met in a vale among the hills. How persuasive was his voice as he told his love! How eloquent his words when he painted the beauties of Nature! Together, we inhaled the refreshing odor of the sea-grass; together, gazed with delight on the silvery flashes which lit up the ocean, and saw ourselves encompassed by the transparent and mysterious haze which arose from it. I called to mind my former hours of solitude and sadness, and, in comparing these memories with the rapture I now enjoyed, I seemed to have found immeasurable happiness. Alas! it was but of short duration. Why must it be that the sun-illumined paths which lead by perfumed shades, and are overhung with a veil of poesy, conduct only to an abyss!

"The summer passed; the autumn came with its yellow leaves and misty mornings. Cold winds blew along the coast, and the angry ocean threw its crested waves against the cliffs. The bathers, true birds of passage, deserted the sea-shore, to return to Paris. Maximin also went, but he did not return. His protestations of love had melted away with the warm breezes of summer, and I was left solitary.

"My loneliness was to me something frightful; and each day seemed interminable, where before, three months had passed almost unconsciously. Braving the wind, the cold, and the rain, I went daily to sit for long hours on the steps of the cross. I still hoped that Maximin would return, but he appeared not.

"There came, at last, a day when I discovered, with mingled emotions of terror and of joy, that I was to become a mother. My courage was aroused; I said to myself, 'I must go seek the father of my child.' I knew not the name of his family, but I resolved to leave my home and look for him in Paris. The only obstacle that restrained me was, the difficulty of finding him; the thought that he might repulse me, and be indifferent to his child, never crossed my mind.

"I secretly quit my father's roof, while the household were wrapped in the slumbers of night. I knelt at the door of my cottage, and stifled the sobs that impeded my prayer. To abandon my mother seemed cruel, but my child demanded my first care. I walked a part of the way on foot, and carried with me only a few light articles of clothing, and my savings in money, sufficient to support me for a year.

"On my arrival in Paris I rented a little furnished chamber under an assumed name.

"I then began my weary search. I had had no idea of the size of Paris; when I surveyed those labyrinths of streets and boulevards, I despaired of ever finding Maximin; I therefore adopted the plan of visiting every day the public promenades. Several months passed, and I had discovered no clew to the object of my search. Finally, one day when I had seated myself, weary and discouraged, on a bench in the Champs Elysées, and was listlessly observing the equipages as they rolled by, on their way to the Bois de Boulogne, my eye caught sight of Maximin, in an elegant cabriolet, drawn by two magnificent blooded horses in tandem. I rose up, and, uttering a loud cry, fell back upon my seat. The carriage rolled on. The footman heard my cry, and looked round at the spot where I was, thus giving me a full view of his person. I noticed also, that he was clad in dark-blue livery, and I fixed all in my memory. Hope revived in my heart. 'I shall find Maximin,' I thought, 'for I now know his servant.'

"I found myself, one evening, near a house in the Faubourg Saint-Honoré, at which the guests were assembling for a party. Placing myself in an angle of the gate-way, and watching the carriages as they passed through into the court, at length I recognized Maximin's footman. I resolved to keep my post, and await the return of the carriage, at the close of the party. My heart beat violently at the thought that so slight an interval of space separated me from my lover.

"The evening wore on. Lights gleamed upon the darkness from the windows of the mansion; but the night was wet and stormy, and gusts of wind rudely shook my frame. What did it matter? My long search was near its close. Two o'clock struck, and the emblazoned carriage, with its liveried footman, was on its return. I followed, and with difficulty kept up with it. Fortunately, the distance was not great, or my strength would have failed me. The carriage turned into the court-yard of a handsome dwelling. After carefully noting the street and the number, I returned to my lodgings.

"I was worn out with fatigue, but my heart was full of joy, for I had found the father of my child. Before removing my wet and mud-stained garments, I knelt down to return thanks to God. I then went to bed and slept profoundly. It was ten o'clock in the morning before I awoke. A faint ray of the sun penetrated my little chamber; I hastily arose and dressed myself in my best clothing. Now, for the first time, anxiety took possession of my heart: Would Maximin know me again? I had suffered so much, and wept so much during the past six months, that my beauty had disappeared like a shadow: I was pale and wasted. I began to tremble, my heart failed me, and I wept. But I said to myself: 'It is not the satisfaction of my love that I seek, but the fulfilment of a duty; not the reclamation of a lover, but the vindication of the name and honor of my child.' I therefore dried my tears, and set out for the residence of Maximin.

"It was noon when I arrived there. Inquiring for the vicomte, the porter directed me to the first door on the second floor. I rang the bell; the valet opened the door, and I entered. Maximin, half reclining upon a divan, was smoking, and reading the morning papers. I stood still, faint, and ready to fall to the floor; perceiving my agitation, he arose and handed me a chair. My veil still covered my face; he had not yet recognized me.

"'What do you wish madame?' said he. I then raised my veil and looked at him. He knew me at once, grew pale, bit his lips, and murmured, 'Valentine!'

"'Yes, it is indeed myself, Maximin, and I have long been seeking you.'

"'So you still remember me, little one? The loves of the summer-time pass when the warm rays of the sun disappear. Those were happy days. It was the most poetic love of my life. I enjoyed some delightful hours, thanks to you, Valentine. I shall always keep the recollection of them fresh in my memory. But what brings you to Paris?'

"'Do you ask such a question? What, indeed, except to find you?"

"'Child, this is unreasonable. Those times have

passed, and I have other occupations now. Meetings such as those of ours on the shore of the ocean, in the midst of the mossy cliffs, would be ridiculous in this great city. You must not think of me, but go back to the green fields of your own country. Besides, the air of the capital does not agree with you—you are pale and suffering.' At this reply, my heart was ready to burst. I arose from my seat, and said quietly to him:

"'Maximin, if you no longer have any love to bestow on me, I shall not importune you for it, but I must nevertheless ask of you a name for your child.' He turned pale again, and stammered out:

"'A name! But young woman, it is not expected that a man should confirm his intrigues with his name; certainly you cannot suppose that. So, you are a mother; well, let us make an agreement; I am an honest man, Valentine, and I will take care of the child. It shall cost you nothing to bring it up, and your situation, too, at the present time, will call for expenses, which I agree to defray myself. But no scandal, I beg of you, or you would displease me, and I could then do nothing more for you.'

"'Then, sir, you will not marry me?'

"'It is out of the question.'

"And you will do nothing to efface the stain that will cling to the career of your child?'

"'I can do nothing.'

"'And will you condemn me to dishonor without pity?'

"'But you see I must.'

"I threw myself at the feet of the vicomte, and clasping his knees, exclaimed: 'Maximin, in the name of our former love, for the sake of the future of our child, have pity; give me at least some hope.' He withdrew himself from me.

"'Madame, it is useless: no scenes; I have given you warning.' He opened a secretary and drew forth a heavy purse. I arose also, and extended my hand for it.

"'So sir, I can never become your wife?'

"'Never.'

"'This is your final decision?'

"'It is.'

"Throwing the purse with violence at the vicomte's head, I exclaimed: 'Sir, the honor of my family is not to be bartered for money. Thank Heaven, your child shall never know that he is the son of a villain!' He clinched his fists with anger, and I turned toward the door, out of which I passed without once looking behind me. I was still in the anteroom when I heard him say to the servant:

"'If you let that woman in again, I will discharge you!'

"A profound contempt for the vicomte replaced my former love. I returned to my little chamber, with no prospect in the future but a life of shame.

I remained in a state of torpor and depression from which I could not rouse myself until evening.

"I had taken no nourishment. I was suffering from cold, desperation, and the sense of insult. In the night, the pains of childbirth seized me, and I was delivered of my child alone, and without assistance. My poor infant was born prematurely, but was living. When I heard its first faint cries, all a mother's joy inundated my soul; I pressed to my bosom the little forsaken one. But next, dark thoughts entered my mind. I said to myself, 'This child will carry with him, as long as he lives, the stigma of illegitimacy. He is the son of Maximin, and doubtless, will, like his father, be a villain and a wretch.' I pushed the child from me; my nerves were in a tremor, and I took it up again; my fingers contracted round its neck. So feeble was the child that its breath was gone in a moment. When I heard its cries no more, I shuddered with terror. My maternal feelings revived; I held my child near the light, that I might examine it more closely; it had ceased to live. I had killed my son! I gave a cry, and fell fainting."

Here, the unhappy woman burst into sobs, wrung her hands, and covered her head with the bedclothing. Her tears moved my heart; I uncovered her head, and would have caressed her, but she pushed me away, saying: "Madame, I do not merit your pity; cast me off, curse me; I have killed my own child!" She wept a long time. When her emotion had subsided, I asked pardon for having renewed her grief—I rested her head upon my shoulder, and calmed her by kind and consoling words.

Finally, she continued her sad story:

"My cry, and the noise of my fall, were heard. My door was burst open. The police were notified.

A blue mark appeared on the neck of the child; I was interrogated, I confessed all, I was placed under arrest. After receiving the care my situation demanded, I was sent here to St.-Lazare.

"It is now known who I am; my family will have heard for the first time of my fault, and of the crime which followed it. My poor mother, already inconsolable for my disappearance, must have wellnigh died of grief. I now calmly await my sentence, for, whatever punishment justice may decree, it will be less terrible than the remorse which devours my heart."

Poor Valentine! she has a delicate and poetic nature; and at eighteen she is the victim of a seducer!

Our laws punish violence, dear Marie, but they do not punish seduction. Nevertheless, women, however weak and timid, can protect themselves against violence, but they are powerless against seduction. To love is natural to them, and, if some vigilant friend be not near to warn her, the young girl may fall an easy prey to the deceiver. At sixteen, the period of inexperience and of illusions, love is viewed as through a prism, and its dangers are unthought of. Why should not young girls be placed under the protection of the law, until they shall have reached their twenty-first year? If the seducer were either obliged to marry his victim, or were punished, fewer crimes and misfortunes would be heard of.

Not only do our laws, however, not punish the

seducer, but our social-customs encourage him. The woman who scorns and disdains her poor, abandoned sister, welcomes with her most gracious smile the author of the latter's fall; while he, on his part, reckons his triumphs by the number of his victims.

For shame! A woman *fails* in her duty to her sex when she does not scorn him who outrages it. She who does not is either unfeeling or unprincipled, or she is guilty herself.

These were the reflections that naturally passed through my mind in view of poor Valentine's history. Entirely overcome, she had fallen back upon her bed. Her eyes were tearless, for she had already wept them dry, and her face still retained the blush that shame had imprinted there. When I thought her sufficiently composed to listen to me, I spoke to her at length, seeking to sustain her with all the consolations that God authorizes us to offer the penitent sinner. She thanked me with a sad smile. When I had ceased speaking, she fell into a profound slumber, and I left her, quitting her bedside on tiptoe.

August 18*th.*

I often see Valentine, and I love her, for a confidence imparted is a tie that binds two souls. The light of joy shines in her eyes when I make my appearance. To-day, when I carried her some delicacies from my own table, she wept and said: "If I had my child, these choice bits would be for him.

Madame, do you believe that God will pardon me for having taken the life of my child?"

"God can pardon all, because He knows the secrets of all hearts. He knows of what we are made, and we have but to bow to His holy will when He punishes us for our faults."

"Thank you, madame, your words always give me so much comfort; they sound in my ears long after you have left me. At night, I see you in my dreams; only, your face is transfigured, and a ray of light illuminates your forehead; you invariably wear a white robe, and your hair, changed to a flaxen hue, falls in curls upon your shoulders."

I laughed at these fancies of her imagination, but Valentine looked serious and added:

"More still, madame. It seems to me, in my dreams, that you live under the same roof with me, and that we breathe the same atmosphere. At the same time I know well that you come from a distance to visit poor prisoners."

This reflection surprised me, for Valentine is entirely igncrant of who I am. It never had occurred to me to go about the house in any other than my secular dress.

The prisoners generally believe me a "*dame de l'œuvre*," one of those pious ladies of whom you must know, Marie, that there is a number who come to visit the *détenues*, and who interest themselves in behalf of this class, on the occasion of their discharge from St.-Lazare, finding places for them, or procuring them work; in a word, doing what they can to prevent their relapsing into crime.

Unfortunately, this admirable society does not count many members, and its means are too limited. It is to be desired that, in a city like Paris, where there are so many generous souls who pass their lives in giving succor to the unfortunate, this work should be greatly extended and placed under the patronage of some distinguished person.

Would that ladies of wealth and position might take under their protection these poor, unfortunate women! This would be a moral work of immense importance; for those who have fallen into vice only under the pressure of poverty would cling to the magnanimous hand extended to withdraw them from their unhappy condition.

August 19th.

Confined in the "Pistole" is a young lady of distinguished manners and rare beauty. You do not know perhaps what I mean by "Pistole," Marie. By this name certain reserved rooms are known, which are put at the disposition of any *détenue* who is willing to pay twenty centimes, or four sous, a day. The name probably was derived from the fact that formerly these rooms were rented at one pistole a month, a piece of money equivalent to about ten francs. This young woman's name is Clemence. I found her one day bathed in tears, and, when I tried to console her, she replied:

"Madame, my unhappiness is of that nature that

it can end only with my life. I married unfortunately, and nothing can be done about that, but weep in silence. Nevertheless, my husband is an honest man and loves me. But I married him against my will. You would not believe what I have suffered in consequence. I assure you, madame, poverty in a state of freedom is far preferable to riches gained by a union in which the heart has no share."

"Why, then, did you consent to such a marriage."

"I was, in a measure, forced into it, under the plea that it was such a good match. I can tell you my history; it is very simple, and is but the repetition of that of many young girls who marry."

You know, my dear friend, how I love to hear histories; so I seated myself to listen.

STORY OF A "GOOD MATCH."

"I WAS born in a village in one of the provinces. I lost my mother while yet in my cradle. My father was possessed of only moderate means, and was burdened, besides, with a numerous family. Thus, he was forced to marry again. My youth was spent unhappily; a strange woman was seated at our hearth, and took from us all that was left to us, the affection of our father. My brothers and myself very often cried; they remembered the caresses lavished upon us by our good mother, and they taught me to repulse her who had taken that mother's place. They, at an early age, left the paternal roof. I was left alone, and my isolation increased the bitterness of my tears.

"A cousin was my only companion; he had a sweet and sympathetic nature, comprehended my loneliness, and tried to console me. We grew up together. Every day, the estrangement between my father and myself widened and deepened. I experienced the greatest repugnance for my stepmother. I loved no one in the world but Francis. My cousin's early education had been obtained under his father's roof; and, when he went to Paris to complete it, what sadness his departure caused me!

"At sixteen years of age, I was sought in marriage by a gentleman who was rich, and in good standing in society. My step-mother, who had a lively desire to rid herself of me, welcomed this occasion as a piece of good fortune. But this gentleman did not please me in the least; he was much older than myself, and between us Francis's image persistently stood. I at first formally refused to marry him. However, I was alone, and had not strength to fight long against the will of my step-mother, or the insinuations of my father, coupled with the protestations of him who sought my hand. To all my objections, my father replied that, as I had no marriage-portion, I never could expect to find so suitable a match. All ended by my yielding, and I was married.

"Alas! why will a family strive to force uncongenial elements to meet? Are they ignorant that fire and water extinguish one another when brought into contact, and that two opposing shocks of electricity produce thunder, the most terrible of all phenomena?

"From that day, my life has been one long martyrdom. I made use of my fortune without enjoying it, and consumed myself in secret tears. God gave me one immense consolation in my sorrow, the possession of a daughter; and I declare that, if I live, *she* shall never marry against her will.

"In the mean time, for special reasons, my husband was obliged to leave the provinces, and come to live in Paris. By this removal, I was again thrown into the society of my cousin, who had just left the military school of St. Cyr. On finding me married, and the mother of a child, he turned pale with astonishment, for, until now, he was in ignorance of what had occurred in our family. He wished to know if I was happy, and soon comprehended that I was not. My husband received him with suspicion, but, as he was my cousin, he dared not repulse him entirely.

"Meanwhile, my birthday, the event of the year to me, recurred. It was a delicious evening, and I was seated upon a sofa enjoying the twilight, and the sweet, soft air coming through the open windows; the flower-stands were filled with fragrant bouquets, which shed on all sides their intoxicating perfumes; my child was playing upon a cushion at my feet. I thought of the sad past, and the future so full of danger, until I was tired of life. The thoughts of Francis so filled my heart that I no longer dared to interrogate it. Marguerite crept upon my knees, and I stroked her silken curls.

"The bell rang; it was Francis. My daughter shouted with joy on seeing him, while I tried to quiet the beating of my own heart. In taking Marguerite from my arms, his hand slightly touched my shoulder; it was unfortunate. Looking around the room, he asked:

"'Why all these flowers to-day?'

"'It is my birthday, and that is the reason

my husband has had these flowers placed in my vases!'

"He bit his lips, and said:

"'He has done his duty. I had forgotten the day, as I forget every thing in my trouble.'

"'You troubled, Francis?'

"'Yes. But what does that signify, if your own days run smoothly on, under an unclouded sky?'

"I hung down my head, and he continued:

"'If I were sure that you are happy, if I saw you gay and smiling, I could be resigned to any thing, even to never seeing you again. But there are moments when your lips tremble, and your cheeks grow pale; when your eyes, which had sparkled with joy on beholding Marguerite, become dull and passionless on turning to your husband. Clemence, I have observed you for a long time; you are a valiant soul, for you suffer without complaining. What a misfortune that you are married!'

"I had not the strength to reply, and he continued:

"'Do you remember the sweet years of our youth, and our happy sports upon the green sward? You have acted very weakly; if I had not left you, you would now have been free.'

"I began to sob. He continued:

"'And this is the end of it—under a gilded exterior, you hide secret unhappiness. Is it not so?'

"He took my hand and covered it with kisses.

"I made no reply. He added:

"'I was poor, like yourself, Clemence, and I had nothing but my sword, but, if you had waited, you might have been happier than you are now.'

"'Yes,' murmured I.

"He looked at me steadily, and asked—

"'Why did you marry, then?'

"'I was compelled to. You know I was but sixteen years old.'

"'My poor friend, have you suffered much?

"'Yes.'

"I withdrew my hand from his, and covered my face.

"My little daughter said:

"'Mamma, what makes you cry?'

"I only replied:

"'Come, my child, and kiss me.'"

"Marguerite encircled my neck with one of her little arms, while she threw the other round the neck of my cousin. His hair and mine commingled, and he said to me in a low voice:

"'Clemence, how much thou art loved!'

"My only response was, to embrace my daughter.

"My cousin covered the place of my kisses upon her cheeks with his own.

"The sight of Francis, which had once proved only an agreeable distraction to my troubles, now served only to increase them; for, from that time, my life was one of anxiety and apprehension. I had a double task to perform, in soothing my cousin, and quieting my husband's suspicions. But I felt misgivings, also, that all was not quite right with my own heart. The presence of my child was the sole mitigation to my distress, and sometimes even she increased my danger. Marguerite and Francis loved each other so much, that they became inseparable. At one time I entertained the thought of repelling my cousin from me. How true it is that a married woman can have no *real* joys outside of her home!

"One day, as I was alone in the parlor, Francis suddenly made his appearance, and said: 'Clemence, I must leave you; I have received orders to join my regiment, and I come to bid you adieu. My God, what it costs me to do so!' This sudden announcement deprived me of all courage; my self-possession abandoned me, and I burst into tears. How conflicting at times are the emotions of the human heart! I had desired a separation from him, and, now that it was about to be accomplished, I was in despair! I advanced toward Francis and said:

"'How can you go away, and leave me alone with this man whom I fear?'

"He replied:

"'Cousin, I have long been trying to think of some means of dissolving this odious tie of yours. Will you follow me? We will carry Marguerite with us. I will wrap her in my cloak, and you shall both be so well concealed that *he* never will be able to trace us.'

"I put my hand over his mouth.

"'Hush, hush!' cried I, 'how can you dare propose such a thing to me! Would you wish to plunge me into infamy and disgrace—to inflict a stain upon the name of my husband, and a stigma on the honor of my child? No, I prefer death, where I am.'

"'It is not death that awaits you here, but something worse, a life endured with one who only makes you wretched.'

"'Do not accuse my husband,' replied I; 'it is you and I alone who are to blame. Go, Francis; I will resign myself to my fate, I will fulfil to the utmost my duties as a wife. I but hope I may soon die.'

"My cousin threw himself at my feet, and besought me with tears to consent to his proposals. I was overwhelmed with anguish; I anathematized society that gives sanction to such unions as that of mine. I was about to seek refuge near my child, that I might strengthen my courage. As I rose, my eyes caught sight, in a mirror before me, of a face that terrified me. My husband had entered the room, unknown to us, and had been a witness to a part of this scene!

"He stood motionless, his fists clinched, his face pale, and his eyes flashing fire. I uttered a cry of dismay. Francis turned and saw my husband, who closed the door behind him, and advanced.

"'Sir,' said he, 'you have come to my house like a thief, to rob me of my honor. When we encounter a robber, we may deal promptly with him. Defend yourself! I rushed toward my cousin, and cried—

"'Francis, swear to me that you will not lift weapons against the father of my child!'

"He hesitated for a moment, and replied:

"'I swear it, upon my sword.'

"Then, turning toward my husband, he crossed his arms upon his breast, and said to him:

"'You are defending your rights, sir; I await your revenge.'

"My husband held menacingly in his right hand a poniard which he often carried on his person. I fell on my knees before him, and exclaimed:

"'Must you become an assassin, because I am unfortunate?'

"He pushed me from him.

"'Defend yourself!' cried he to Francis, who remained motionless. Finally, he opened the door, and said to my cousin:

"'Then, you can leave; you are a villain!' Francis wavered at this insult, and turned toward me.

"'Poor Clemence! poor victim!' murmured he, and slowly withdrew.

"The frightened domestics had crowded into the anteroom at the noise of the altercation, and cast anxious and curious glances into the parlor. I flew to my chamber. My husband, following me, said:

"'Madame, make your preparations. You will soon set out on a long journey,' and then left me. Frightful presentiments filled my heart. I had Marguerite brought to me, and I held her for a long time closely pressed to my bosom.

"In one hour after my husband returned, and bade me embrace my daughter for the last time. My knees gave way under me, and I fell prostrate upon the floor, exclaiming:

"'Have mercy! I am not guilty of crime; do not take my child from me.' He smiled a bitter smile, and, in spite of my efforts and Marguerite's cries, he tore her from my arms and put her into the hands of a maid, who took her away.

"I soon heard the rumbling of a carriage in the street, leaving the house. Hardly was the noise lost in the distance, than he said to me, 'Now for us two, madame.' Then, throwing a cloak over my shoulders, and placing the hood of it over my head, he led me away. I was overwhelmed with grief and anxiety, not for myself, but for my child. However, I unresistingly followed him.

"A carriage was waiting for us at the door, which we entered. The coachman immediately touched off his horses, and, traversing a multitude of small streets, brought us out upon the quays. We crossed a bridge, and soon after the carriage stopped; we were at the office of the chief of police. My husband descended, and his place was taken by an officer. The carriage moved on again. Rousing myself from my stupor, I tried to open the door. I cried out:

"'My husband, my child!' The officer drew me back, shut the windows, closed the curtains, and said to me:

"'Madame, keep quiet.'

"'Where are we going?' said I.

"'You will soon learn,' he replied.

"When the carriage stopped, I found myself inside the court of St.-Lazare, and before a door partially grated and bearing the inscription:

"PREMIÈRE SECTION.
PRÉVENUES.—CONDAMNÉES."

"The officer gave a light stroke with the knocker, and the keepers appeared. My conductor held in his hand a note, which he gave to the 'brigadier.' It read: 'To be confined by order of her husband. (*Pistole.*)' I was then shown into the registry, where my name was entered, after which I returned to the vestibule.

"A keeper gave a signal by one stroke of a bell, and then, placing his lips at a tube, uttered the words, 'A prisoner.' A flight of stairs was pointed out to me; I ascended to the floor above, where I was received by a sister. She rang another bell, and repeated, at a tube, the same words, 'A prisoner.' Again I was desired to go a story higher; which I did, and entered a room unfurnished except by benches. From this room a door opened to the left, with the word '*vestiaire*' written upon it. An aged woman, dressed in black, stood at the door and invited me in. She was the clothes-keeper of the establishment.

"I complied, and found myself in a square chamber, the walls of which were covered with cases or shelves, divided into regularly-numbered compartments for clothing. A table occupied the centre of the room, on which lay a large open book.

"'Madame, will you give me your jewels?' said the old lady. I immediately gave her my finger-rings, ear-rings, and watch.

"'Have you any money?' I gave her my porte-monnaie, which she opened and found to contain fifty francs. Ten of these she handed back to me, saying:

"'Madame, the remainder of your money, as also your jewels, will now be deposited in the office of registration, and will be returned to you when you leave the prison.' She then gathered them all up and wrote the list in the large book upon the table. She proceeded to search my person. Finding nothing and perceiving my blushes, she said:

"'Pardon me, madame, I have only fulfilled my indispensable duty, which is now finished, and you can go below.'

"On the floor below I encountered the same sister to whom the officer from Paris had given the note on my entrance, and which she still held in her hand. In silence she conducted me through a long corridor, indicated my cell to me, and fastened the door securely after me.

"I do not know what has become of Francis, nor has my husband been to see me; and three months have now passed since I gave the last embrace to my child."

Here the unhappy mother covered her face with her hands, and a torrent of tears streamed from her eyes. I let her exhaust her grief for a time, and cast my eyes round her room. It contained four small beds, for in this portion of St.-Lazare there are no single cells. The coarsely-whitewashed walls were destitute of ornament, the grated window looked out only upon one of the court-yards, and the room was destitute of furniture except a few wooden stools painted brown, a small table, and in each corner of the room an earthen pitcher. I thought of the privations this delicate woman, who had been taken from a sumptuous home, must endure in a place like this. Thinking to divert her mind from its sad thoughts, I said to her:

"Madame, I sympathize with your feelings; the nakedness and solitude here must be very depressing to you."

"She shook her head and replied:

"No, for solitude restores me to liberty: I am far from my husband, and I breathe freely. Poverty does not frighten me; I have not always been rich. Would to God my father had taught me some trade or occupation by which I might have earned my living, and then he never could have been able to marry me against my will! I should have been poor but happy, instead of being rich and a prisoner. Here is what this fine marriage, so much extolled by my step-mother, has brought me to: I am in St.-Lazare, and the associate of prostitutes!" As she said this her lips grew pale, and the color mounted to her face.

"Your husband," remarked I, "has certainly used extreme measures. But may it not be through your own fault? He *believes* you guilty, at least, and you did not defend yourself as you should from the imputation."

"I am not, it is true, guilty of the crime which he imputes to me; but, why should I try to excuse myself, when adultery was in my heart? I do not love my husband. I do love another; therefore, I merit my punishment."

"Have you no fear that your affair may become a public scandal?"

Smiling sadly, she replied:

"My husband is very prudent; he knows how to preserve the honor of his name: I have no fear for that. He will say that I have been to a watering-place, or on a journey; and, should it please him some day to recall me to his house, he will prepare a feast in honor of my return. Splendid toilets will crowd my apartments; my parlors will be filled with my friends; he will force me to rouge my cheeks, oblige me to dry my tears and to smile upon those who come to welcome my return. Ah! if I had my child, how much more I would prefer my prison-life!"

I reflected for a moment, and asked her:

"Have you written to your husband while here?"

"Never."

"You must write to him."

"Why?"

"To ask him about Marguerite."

"Will you take charge of the letter, and convey it to him?"

"I cannot; the rules of the house forbid it."

"Then I shall not write, because my letter would be read by the recorder."

"Of what consequence is that to you?"

"It is of great consequence; we must keep our sad secret to ourselves."

"You may be sure that the secrets of St.-Lazare are well kept."

She supplicatingly joined her hands, and said, weeping:

"Madame, how grateful I would be to you, if you could bring me some information of my child!"

At this moment the great bell announced the hour of dinner. I rose to go, but put my finger on my lips, and whispered:

"Be of good cheer, I will see you again."

Marriage is a grave affair. To a woman, the consequences, be they good or bad, are permanent. Yet, in France, they marry between the ages of sixteen and eighteen! Where is there one that has acquainted herself, before marriage, with the laws that bear upon that condition? Not one. She unites her destiny, then, to that of a stranger, without comprehending the extent of the obligations she contracts, or the weight of the yoke to which she will have to submit. For this reason, I am constrained to compassionate all married women who find their condition an unhappy one, as also to palliate their errors, if they commit any.

Let a woman be married at the age of twenty-one, when her reason is fully developed; but first place in her hands a book explaining the legal condition of a wife, and, after she has perused it attentively, then ask her if she is willing to contract marriage. If she assents, she will understand, also, that she accepts all the consequences of her decision. But, do not permit her to bind herself irrevocably, without knowing the nature of the step she is to take. Do not take from her her fortune, her will, her liberty, without this full appreciation on her part of her condition. If you do, be not astonished at her subsequent revolt, her wild resistance to her lot, and the many faults of which she will become guilty!

August 20th.

Valentine has recovered sufficiently to be out of bed. She came forward to receive me, but was so feeble that I obliged her to be seated again.

"I have passed a bad night," she said. "I saw him again."

"Whom did you see, pray?"

"The vicomte."

"You must forget him, my child."

"If you could know how I despise him! But I had a fever yesterday; I dreamed, though half awake, that I saw Maximin at a party, in a large drawing-room brilliantly lighted, and decorated with flowers, golden candelabra, and silk drapery. He was surrounded by a great many beautiful young ladies, very elegantly dressed. Maximin came and went, smiling alike upon all, and smiled upon by all. He stopped suddenly, and fixed a burning glance upon a young girl, who wore an exquisite toilet of light-blue silk, with a white flower in her dark hair. At this glance, she grew pale, and hung down her head. The eye of the seducer had marked another victim. I made an effort to raise my voice in warning, to cry out: 'Beware of that man! I am one of his victims. He will envelop you in his folds like a serpent, and you will be lost.' But my voice could not force its way through my burning throat.

"Maximin, still with his eyes fixed upon the beautiful stranger, who was now trembling with excitement, slowly advanced toward her. I suffered a thousand deaths at the spectacle, for I well remembered the power of his glance. At the moment when, with quivering lips, the girl advanced in her turn toward the vicomte, and extended her hand to him, I made a last despairing effort to speak, and succeeded. The words that escaped my lips immediately appeared in letters of fire upon the seducer's forehead. I then came to myself. In an instant, flowers, drapery, candelabra, Maximin, the young girl, all had disappeared. I found a religious standing by the side of my bed, who, taking my hand in hers, said: 'Valentine, my child, you are in suffering. You must try to keep calm, and get some sleep.' I believe I had really cried out, in my half-waking slumbers.

"When I lie awake at night, and reflect upon where I am, how the sight of these walls depresses me! How gloomy the light of the flickering night-lamp! Ah, madame, if women who are virtuous only knew what remorse and suffering follow in the train of vice, never would they allow themselves to be led astray! You, whose voice may perhaps reach others, speak in my behalf, and tell the story of my wretchedness, that my example may be a warning to my sex."

Marie, the grief of this poor girl moves me most deeply, and, when I see her weep, it is with difficulty that I can restrain my own tears.

August 22d.

I returned to my chamber, overcome with sadness. I felt, within my own heart, as though the concentrated griefs of all women had entered there, so much had I heard of their sorrows, open and secret. If Valentine's future days should be spent in a condition of humiliation and expiation, still, she will be in one sense free—she will not be bound to another. But Clemence is irrevocably joined to a man she can never love! I threw myself upon my bed, in a state of weariness, and, while endeavoring to think of some means of ameliorating the condition of women, I fell into a feverish and agitated slumber, in which I had a dream, which I will proceed to relate.

THE VISION.

I SAW an immense plain, naked, sterile, and deserted, with here and there a little green grass growing on the borders of innumerable paths cut in the rocks. Daylight was approaching, but was as yet scarcely perceptible, the sky was gloomy and covered with clouds; not one star shone through the darkness.

Suddenly, a multitude of women made their appearance; they came from the East, the West, the South, and the North. All of these women wore long black mantles, and their faces were concealed by a veil of the same color. They advanced slowly, almost bowed to the ground, apparently walking with the greatest difficulty. A sound that seemed like the rattling of chains accompanied their movements.

After them, young girls dressed in white, and crowned with roses, sportively advanced. In an instant, the entire plain was covered by this multitude, and all seated themselves on the ground, except the young girls, who continued their gambols. Suddenly, a loud voice was heard, like the roaring of a cataract in a tempest. Raising my eyes, I perceived an airy figure descending from the clouds. Hovering over the assembly, it uttered these words:

"O wives, sighing in hopeless dependence, awaken to the reality of your condition, and contemplate it as it truly is. Behold, the yoke of man weighs heavily upon you, because you look to him alone for your daily sustenance, and your hearts resent this dependence. If you would enjoy freedom, then, learn to labor."

At these words, the women who were seated rose up; the others ceased their diversion, and all took an attitude of attention. The voice continued:

"Yes, Nature indeed deals harshly with you. Man, in coming into the world, rends your womb; in infancy, he wounds your breast; in maturity he breaks your heart."

Then the elder women cried out:

"But, must he always break our hearts?"

And the younger exclaimed, with astonishment:

"Mothers, is it true you suffer thus? These are sorrows we never suspected."

Then the mothers, with a mournful smile, opened their garments, and displayed over the place of the heart a bloody stigma. The young girls started back appalled, and, snatching from their heads their crowns of roses, cast them upon the ground, crying out:

"Poor mothers! we will leave our sports, to join our tears with yours."

The figure continued:

"God has created woman to be the companion of man, to be the flesh of his flesh, and the bone of his bone. Be such, therefore, but never consent to be his plaything nor his slave. If God must punish despotism in man, he must also punish weakness in woman. O woman! awaken from thy deadly state! It is time that thy slavery were at an end!"

"Shall we still be able," cried they, "to retrieve some portion of the liberty we have lost?"

The celestial figure replied:

"In wedlock, man and woman are but parts of one whole, they should therefore harmonize one with the other. Nothing is to be gained by resistance; give yourselves to prayer, and God will support you; labor, and your sufferings will be alleviated; cast your eyes up to heaven, and the evils of this world will disappear. But, if nothing is left to you, except to bow your heads and hide the tears that flow, there is still a work for you to accomplish for your daughters: they must entitle themselves to independence by an early application to labor, so that they may be in a condition to choose their own husbands, and not, like you, be condemned to a future of sorrow."

The mothers, laying their hands upon the heads of the young girls, said:

"We solemnly promise that our daughters, secured in their independence by their familiarity with labor, shall earn the liberty to choose their own husbands."

Once more the voice spoke:

"O woman, arise from your servitude, and let labor set you free!"

Then the figure disappeared in space, leaving the echo of its parting words to be caught up and repeated by future generations of women, as the password to happiness: "*Let labor set you free!*" A ray of sunlight spread over the plain; and the phantoms of my vision vanished.

I awoke, panting and oppressed; involuntarily, I laid my hand on my heart: it was not wounded exteriorly, it had only suffered interiorly from the wounds of others. I threw around me a morning-wrapper, and, without pausing to gather up my hair, which hung loosely over my shoulders, I went to lean on the sill of my window to breathe the fresh air. My blinds were open, and I was listening to the great clock as it sounded the hour of eight, when I heard a cry in the court below.

The prison-van was there, and one of the inmates was supplicatingly extending her arms toward me, crying out:

"My dream, O my dream!"

It was Valentine! She had been tried the night before, and condemned to three years' imprisonment, and was now about to be carried to the central prison, to expiate her sentence. She waved a last adieu, and the keeper led her away. I never saw her more.

As to Maximin, he is enjoying, I learned, this world's happiness; he is admired and feasted, and is about to marry a rich heiress.

August 23d.

The departure of Valentine saddened me; besides, these walls, these gratings, oppress my heart; I cannot habituate myself to them. To change the scene, I walked out, so that, by withdrawing from St.-Lazare, I might forget it for a time at least. I picked up a book at random, and directed my steps toward a little quiet walk that I had discovered outside the walls. I had been for some ten minutes seated on a bench, when an aged lady, of a very respectable appearance, leaning upon the arm of a distinguished-looking young man, apparently her son, came and took a seat at my side. The gentleman, after saluting me, seated himself near his mother. At this moment my book fell from my lap to the ground. The young gentleman very politely picked it up and returned it to me. At the same time, looking at the title, he remarked:

"Madame, you are reading M. de ——?"

"Yes, sir," I replied.

"Do you admire his style?"

"Very much—he is my favorite author."

"How so? Is it because you know him personally?"

"No, sir."

"*I* have seen him, and even spoken to him," remarked he.

"And what do *you* think of him?"

"I esteem him; he is a clever man, but very odd; in that particular he resembles his class. You know all literary people are peculiar."

"Do you think so?" I inquired.

"Assuredly, madame; are you not acquainted with literary people?"

I evaded a reply, and he resumed:

"It is easy to discern that you have never been familiar with the princes of the inkhorn. Allow me to compliment you on that point, madame, for in their company we are always in danger of losing the plain good sense with which Nature has endowed us. Place a literary man in the midst of twenty persons of various conditions in life, and you will distinguish him immediately from all others: he will either have his cravat wrong side out, or a lock of rebellious hair menacing the sky, or there will be something in his manner or dress different from others."

I commenced to laugh, and said:

"Since you say so, sir, I must believe you; but you surprise me. I had thought, until now, that men of letters were like other men."

At this the lady remarked:

"My son has an aversion for literary persons, but he goes too far. I can excuse him for his detesting authoresses; in that he does well, but as to men, authorship is an honorable calling for them."

The young man tapped the heel of his polished boot with his cane, and resumed:

"Female authors! Blue-stockings! Bah! They are folly personified. One may discover them still more readily than male authors, by their positive style of gait, and their eccentric toilets.—You, madame, who are attired so simply and naturally, must have been especially struck by their oddities."

I laughed in my sleeve, but made no reply. The gentleman soon commenced walking to and fro near us. The old lady regarded him with eyes of affection.

"My son is handsome, and talks well, does he not?" said she to me.

"Madame, you are unquestionably a happy mother."

"Pardon me my admiration for him," she replied; "he is my only earthly joy. He is such a good son! I hope God will return to him all the happiness he has been the means of bestowing upon his mother," and some tears escaped her. She continued:

"I have only one desire, and that is, to see him united to a companion worthy of him before I die. I have given him full permission to marry, but he evinces no inclination to do so. I desire that no considerations of fortune or of birth should influence him. Provided his wife be virtuous and gentle, and will always consult his happiness, I shall be content. But he is not easily pleased; he is free to choose, and is independent in his circumstances, nay, is rich. May God give him wisdom, and may he be happy!"

The young man turned again toward us, and the mother ceased to speak. To hear this unknown woman speak so tenderly of her son, moved me. We parted.

September 15th.

I was tired of writing, and I laid aside my manuscript to seek a little recreation. I went out every day to walk on my favorite promenade. It is an unfrequented spot, overlooking the Strasbourg Railroad depot from the west. There I often met the old lady referred to in my last letter. On such occasions I would close my book, and we would enter into conversation, while she occupied herself with some light needle-work. We always separated with a mutual glance, implying a rendezvous for the next day.

Last week the lady did not meet me, as usual, and I concluded that she was either sick or absent; but yesterday, just as I was about leaving, she made her appearance. She was pale, and in those few days had grown older in appearance by several years. She came toward me, and sat down, almost overcome with agitation, upon the bench beside me, saying:

"I was looking for you, madame, and undoubtedly I shall appear to you very indiscreet and absurd, but you will have compassion upon a poor old mother, and answer my questions. My son is sick, and in danger of death. Last night, during his delirium, I took occasion to interrogate him. He admires you, madame, or rather mademoiselle, for you are not married, are you?" upon which she cast her eyes upon my ungloved hand, to convince herself.

"I am free, madame," I replied.

"My son," she continued, "is desirous of knowing who you are; he has presumed to follow you, that he might ascertain your residence, and he was punished well for his temerity, for he believes he saw you enter St.-Lazare. Reassure him through me, and let me tell him that he was mistaken."

"It is true, madame. I do inhabit the establishment of St.-Lazare."

"Then you admit it, mademoiselle?"

"Yes, madame."

"What a misfortune! My son would have offered you his hand in marriage, whatever might have been your position; but, to a prisoner of St.-Lazare—"

"And who told you I was a prisoner?"

"No one. But then, why are you there in prison?"

"Think a little: prisoners are never allowed to go out."

"That is true, at least, generally speaking. However, there may be privileged characters among the prisoners; for example, ladies of rank, who can have a keeper to follow them at a distance, perhaps. Now, mademoiselle, my son is persuaded that your case is an exceptional one, and in his delirium he talks of nothing but the prison. I know him well; he will die if he is not relieved from his sad impressions," and the poor mother began to weep.

I pitied her, and said:

"Madame, your son appeared to me to be a man of intelligence; how is it that he does not comprehend that there must be others besides prisoners in a house of that kind, and that it is necessary that some one be appointed to oversee and govern, and provide for the inmates; in a word, that functionaries are needed to fulfil these duties?"

The old lady uttered a cry of joy, and, wiping away her tears, seized my hands in a transport of delight.

"Pardon me, mademoiselle, I comprehend: you belong to the family of one of these functionaries. You shall be my daughter, and you shall make my son happy; he is saved; you will not refuse to marry him, will you?" She arose, still continuing: "I will run to carry him this good news, and it will cure him. I ask your pardon for our error—you, a prisoner!"

As she was about to leave, I detained her to say:

"Do not rejoice too soon, madame; your son will never marry me."

"Do you refuse him, then?"

"No; but he will never ask me when he comes to know who I am."

The lady stepped back a little and looked at me with an air of anxiety, saying:

"Who, then, are you?"

"To your son, madame, I should prove more objectionable than a prisoner. I am *an authoress*."

The poor mother sat down upon the bench, confounded, and I profited by her astonishment to descend hurriedly from the terrace and disappear. I laughed at this adventure until I cried. I took care not to return again to the terrace. I should like to know, however, if the young man was cured of his delirium, but I have no idea that he will ever be cured of his dislike to authoresses.

An interruption, occasioned by my being asked for in the parlor, made me drop my pen for a moment. Descending thither, I found a lady plainly dressed in black, and looking very sad. Without speaking, she handed me a sealed note: it was a letter of recommendation. I had before me evidently some great suffering to relieve, but I did not know whether it was a case of destitution, or of misfortune in some other form. While I was reading the note, the poor woman covered her face with her handkerchief: her daughter, I read, is among the prisoners of St.-Lazare!

O mothers, who have not bread to give your children, how often have I wept for you! but to-day I am made acquainted with a wretchedness still more profound. It is that of a mother crushed with shame under the weight of a daughter's disgrace. My heart is broken, Marie; this woman's sorrows have moved my inmost soul; I could not find one word of consolation to give her; but I promised her to watch over her erring child, until the penalties of the law shall be fulfilled in regard to her, and she shall be free to leave the prison.

September 16th.

I found, to-day, one of the inmates seated at the bottom of the stairs, crying with all her heart. To let me pass, she was obliged to move, and I paused to say to her:

"Tell me, young woman, why are you crying so?"

She wiped her eyes with a cambric handkerchief trimmed with lace, and replied:

"I am crying because I have no money to pay the washerwoman, who has taken my linen away as security."

"You must work and earn it, then."

Looking up to me, she said:

"I beg pardon, madame, I thought it was one of the sisters I was speaking to."

As she stood two or three steps from me, arranging her neck-handkerchief very carefully over her bosom, I noticed that she wore the prison costume, with the exception that instead of the "sabots," or wooden shoes, her feet were covered with bootees of rose-colored satin. She continued:

"Madame, we are unlucky; it is all over with us girls, our business is ruined. Certain women, called honest, come too much in competition with us. They, in fact, enjoy more freedom than we do. Law is not always justice; the police hold *us* under surveillance; all right, we do not complain; but they ought, also, to give an eye to *others*. We are forbidden to go out with our heads uncovered, while women of fashion are allowed to show themselves half naked at private balls and at public entertainments; and so, they attract customers that would otherwise come to us."

It was a courtezan who thus spoke, and her words were the most withering rebuke that could possibly be administered to the manners and fashions of our day. This girl was still young, but already faded, and a dark line encircled her lustreless eyes.

"Poor child," said I, "would you not do better to abandon a life so criminal and low?"

"It is impossible, madame; once engaged in this manner of living, we must follow it to the end. We live outside the pale of society: honest people keep aloof from us; no one will furnish us with work; we must keep on as we have begun, or else die of hunger on the streets."

Alas! perhaps there is too much truth in what she says. I left her and passed on.

September 17th.

Do not suppose, dear friend, that the entire population of St.-Lazare is supplied by Paris alone. The provinces also send thither a large number. Multitudes of young girls from the different departments of France enter the capital, only to be lost. They come to Paris in search of work, and they encounter only corruption. They come thither, virtuous, and ignorant of evil, but poverty overtakes them, and temptation leads them astray. The result is, that they finally find their way here. If the people of the provinces only knew Paris as it is, never would they send their children there. Boys may pass unharmed, perhaps, but girls . . . !

Why leave the country, with its pure air, its bright sun, its broad liberty, and its modest gains, which are, after all, sufficient to supply all necessaries, in order to repair to this great city, where the air is so gross, where work is often so difficult to find, and where life is worn out so quickly? The attraction is the prospect of making a little money; but, for one that becomes better off, how many there are who drag out their lives in poverty? It is frightful to think of the numberless dangers that young persons who are alone, inexperienced, and exposed to so many temptations, incur.

A young woman, well brought up, once set out from her home in the country, for Paris, where she was to live with an aunt. Her mother was imprudent enough to permit her to travel alone, because it had been arranged, previously, that her friends should be in waiting for her on her arrival at the station in Paris. In the course of the journey, a slight accident occurred, so that the cars, instead of arriving at eight o'clock in the evening, did not reach Paris until eleven. Not expecting the train at so late an hour, her friends had not waited for it; she found herself, therefore, on her arrival, alone, and in a position of great embarrassment. A gentleman, seeing her perplexity, addressed her very politely, and offered her accommodations for the night. The poor child accepted the delusive hospitality offered. The next day, the police arrested her, and now she is in St.-Lazare. Her mother will long repent the imprudence of which she was guilty.

There are women, too, whose base calling it is to attend railroad-stations, to waylay young girls, and bring them to houses of perdition. They offer them work, which the poor creatures gladly accept, only to embrace dishonor. Those infamous houses called "*maisons de tolérance*" depend almost entirely on stratagem for recruiting their inmates, and this in spite of the active vigilance of the authorities. In every place where numbers of young girls may be met with are to be found those terrible harpies, the proprietors of such houses, hovering around in search of victims.

How it pains me to write these lines, Marie; these are details that revolt and sadden me. Pardon me for setting them before you; I do so because I judge them useful. We must know where the evil is, in order to be able to battle against it. It is necessary to warn young persons of the dangers in their path, of which they are ignorant, in order that they may take means of escaping them. They should learn that, in their case, distrust is the mother of security.

As I was passing through the corridor appropriated to those who have undergone sentence, I perceived a convict standing apart from the others; her lips were tightly compressed, and her eyes fixed upon the ground; her cheeks wore a sickly pallor, and her dejected countenance betrayed deep trouble.

For an instant I experienced toward her a feeling of involuntary aversion. When the sister saw me looking at her, she said to me:

"That is one of the class called *transferred*" (*transferées*).

"How transferred?"

"This one, for instance, after awaiting her trial for three months, has been condemned to two years' incarceration in the central prison. She is now awaiting removal. Sometimes the exigencies of the service occasion a delay of eight to fifteen days after their trial, before the prisoners really undergo transfer, and during this period they may be sent for at any hour of the day or night. The vehicle in which they are placed contains separate locked compartments, and each prisoner is supplied with bread for the journey, be the journey long or short, for she is not allowed to leave the prison-carriage until her destination is reached. You may easily recognize this carriage, from its being painted a maroon-color; it is ventilated at top, but has no windows. One officer sits within, and a single driver occupies the box. If part of the journey be by rail, the carriage is placed on a truck, and thus proceeds on its way without further derangement."

I thanked the sister for these details, and desired to know the crime of this particular *transferée.* It seems that an interesting history is connected with the crime of this odious creature.

I will relate it to you:

THE SNARE.

Adeline was a girl of eighteen, tall and beautiful in figure. Her life had been passed in a little village, in the south of France. Her father was a man of superior mind, and of deep learning, and she was his only child. He had himself undertaken the care of his daughter's education, but the study of the sciences alone was not entirely to the taste of Adeline, who found much difficulty in applying herself to her books; she preferred free life in the open air, a life of independence and adventure among her native mountains. Her father's possessions lay at the foot of the Pyrenees, or rather in a gorge of those mountains, where he had built a charming villa, in which he was accustomed to pass the summer months. Adeline accompanied her father in the chase, and in his long walks, and thus became familiar with the torrents, abysses, and precipices, with which those mountain-passes abound.

Her father would carry her books in a small travelling-satchel, which the scholar would leave in the crevices of some rock, and readily forget. She preferred to study the azure sky, or the lofty mountains—to admire the pines, spreading their great arms across the ravines, or the wild-flowers which exhaled their sweet perfume beside the laughing waters of the cascade. More agile than the chamois, she climbed the steepest rocks, and leaped the fissures; then, running until out of breath, she would suddenly pause to await the arrival of her father. She would next seat herself upon the carpet of grass, and call to mind the forgotten books, the lessons she had promised to learn.

The father arriving, would bring the books which he had perhaps found by mere chance, where she had left them; choosing the vicinity of a limpid stream, they would breakfast with an appetite which the pure air of the mountains alone could create. The master commenced his lessons, asking questions and furnishing the replies himself. Or, learnedly expatiating on the phenomena of Nature, he would describe the formation of the primitive rocks, the mysteries of electricity, or the laws that govern the atmospheric currents, and the like.

Finding the child's attention fixed, the father would continue:

"In Paris, the capital of France, there are schools where all the sciences are taught; there, are to be found men who have measured the heights of our mountains, analyzed the waters of our springs, classified our animals and rocks."

The child, before so gay and playful, would now become pensive, and say to herself:

"Science is but of little avail to me, I can never comprehend it; but how I should like to know those learned men—to see Paris!"

Thus the man made himself a child, and the child aspired to maturity, and both would enter into deep reveries, until the sun, fast sinking behind the high mountains, gave them warning that it was time to return to the villa.

Resuming their way by paths scarcely perceptible, they would reach home, overcome with fatigue, but so happy! Adeline, as she entered the garden-walks of their home, would meet her mother, a gentle creature, who complained to her husband that he was rearing the child like a peasant.

After a joyful embrace, the mother would reprove her for her disordered dress, and contemplate with dismay her sunburnt hands and face. Adeline, returning her caresses, would laughingly receive her mild complaints, and promise to be more careful of herself in future, but afterward give occasion on the first opportunity, for renewed expostulation.

Such was the manner of life led among the mountains, until a breach in the fortunes of the family brought about a change. The father was obliged to sell his pretty villa, and Adeline said to herself:

"My father and mother, with their little remnant of fortune, will be able to live comfortably, but I should be a heavy charge on them: I must go and earn my own living."

She was by nature self-reliant and courageous; in one night her course was determined upon.

Adeline knew a former resident of the neighborhood, who had long lived in Paris, and who at rare intervals returned to visit her native village. On these occasions her exterior was that of one in opulent circumstances, and it was said that she had made a large fortune in the silk-trade. Adeline quietly procured her address, and wrote to her, soliciting an engagement, or any employment whatever. An answer was soon received, promising a lucrative position immediately. Foreseeing the resistance that her father and mother would naturally make to this arrangement, the young girl left her home without notifying them of her intentions, charging a friend to break the news when she should be far away.

It was evening when she arrived in the capital, and the old lady, according to agreement, was at the station to meet her. Taking Adeline by the hand, she led her beneath the light of a street-lamp, and took a rapid survey of her; she was struck with her beauty. They immediately entered a carriage in waiting, and were conveyed to a mansion of elegant appearance.

Entering here, Adeline found apartments furnished with every luxury, and was shown to a chamber for herself, in keeping with the rest, where a good dinner was shortly served up to her on a little table. Adeline dined alone, and ate but little: the appearance of her lady-friend did not please her; she felt in her heart an inexpressible misgiving on first entering the house. The memories of her home and her childhood passed through her mind, clothed in vivid colors; she looked around her and reflected how much more beautiful was the green carpet of the Pyrenees than the splendor of the Wilton beneath her feet.

While the tears were flowing at the thought of her dear mother, the mistress of the house came in to see her. She embraced her affectionately, and urged her to retire, and give herself the repose she needed. An old servant-maid, coming to do the work of the room, glanced at her curiously. The latter was soon dismissed, and her mistress shortly followed. Then the young girl threw herself upon her knees, said her prayers as usual, and lay down to rest.

Her sleep was troubled; the silk drapery of her alcove appeared to stifle her. Two or three times she suddenly awoke and sat up in bed, to listen. She thought she distinguished sounds of laughter, the clinking of glasses, in short, all the indications of a midnight revel in progress. When she fell asleep again, she was visited by sinister dreams.

At the return of day, no sound was to be heard throughout the house. Adeline arose, and, looking for her clothes, perceived that the servant had taken away her dress and shawl. In place of the former, she found a morning-gown of white silk, trimmed with rose-colored ribbon, spread out over an arm-chair, but she would not touch it. Dressing herself as she best could in her remaining garments, and throwing her night-dress over her, she went to the door. Finding it locked, she rang the bell, and sat down on the side of the bed to await a reply. The maid-servant appeared, bringing a waiter with coffee, rolls, and butter. A little silver-handled knife, with a pointed steel blade, lay beside her plate.

"I want my dress," said Adeline to her.

"Mademoiselle," said she, "it was very much soiled by travel. Will you not have the kindness, meanwhile, to put on this morning-gown? Madame will soon rise, and then orders will be given to have your trunk opened."

The old woman left the room, but Adeline had no wish for food. She buried her face in her hands, and began to ponder deeply. While thus occupied, the door was noiselessly opened, and a stranger glided into the room. His hat was on his head, he had a cigar in his mouth, and he coolly seated himself in a chair, and crossed his legs. Slight as was the noise made by his entrance, Adeline perceived it, and looked up. While she regarded the stranger with a look of stupefaction, he on his part inspected her attentively. Her black hair hung in profusion over her white shoulders, which no vulgar gaze had ever before rested on; her eyes, slightly distended by alarm, flashed also with indignation, and her half-opened lips curled with disdain.

"Sir," said Adeline, "by what right do you dare enter my chamber?"

The stranger only replied:

"They have not deceived me. You are indeed a marvel of beauty."

The young girl drew her night-dress closely round her, and, stepping before the stranger, said to him:

"Sir, leave my room!"

"Oh! by no means. I am at home, here, as well as you."

"Then," replied Adeline, "I shall leave you in possession," and, hastening to the door, tried to open it. Impossible, it was securely fastened from without. A giddiness seized Adeline, and, overcome with terror, she commenced to cry aloud for help.

"Now, young woman, a little less noise, if you please. Well, the crazy fit is on; I shall wait until it is over."

"I am not crazy."

"Then you are playing the honest woman; we know all about that."

At these words a horrible thought crossed the mind of the young girl. She turned to the stranger, and said, appealingly:

"Sir, have you a sister, or a mother? Then, in the name of that mother, tell me in what house I am! What place is this?"

At the bottom of the vilest heart there is always a silent chord that responds to the remembrance of a mother, and awakens in the heart better impulses, at least for the moment. The stranger took his hat from his head, and, bowing respectfully, replied:

"We are in a house, to which the approach, even, is interdicted to respectable females, miss."

"You are an honest man, sir. You will save me,

protect me, and aid me to leave this house. I have been brought here through an infamous plot. I have just arrived in Paris. I am a stranger, and not wicked. I am an honorable girl. Have pity upon me!"

At this, the stranger seated himself again, saying:

"Miss, you play your part with all the skill of an accomplished tragedienne. You could make your fortune on the stage. Even were this all true, no one would believe you. Upon my word, you are too handsome."

At these words, the fears of Adeline gave place to the courage of the child of the mountains. She bounded toward the door, seized the knob, and shook it violently, but without avail; she then endeavored to reach the window, but the stranger barred the passage. At this she uttered shrill cries, but her cries received no answer. The stranger approached her. The young girl drew back against the wall, and casting a look of despair around the room, caught sight of the little knife lying on the table. She seized it, and raising it, exclaimed:

"Sir, if you advance one step nearer, I will plant this knife in your heart!"

There was an air of such energetic resolution in her gesture and manner, and in the tone of her voice, that the stranger drew back, judging it not prudent to attempt further aggression. He gave two knocks on the door, which caused it to open immediately, and he withdrew without loss of time. In passing through the house, he met its mistress.

"Take care of yourself, old woman," cried he; "you are making business for the police."

Meanwhile, Adeline, finding herself free, hastily followed, resolved on escape. The house, so lately in profound quiet, was now entirely aroused, and at every door Adeline encountered fresh obstacles to her exit. Pushing aside whomsoever impeded her path, she made her way into the street, half clad, with hair dishevelled, and almost beside herself with anger and terror.

It was but eight in the morning, and directly opposite the dwelling was a shop, which was just being opened for the business of the day. The poor girl startled the assistants as if a bomb-shell had fallen among them, by her sudden appearance in their midst. She requested shelter and protection: the young women of the establishment surrounded her immediately, and supplied her with requisite clothing, after which the police were sent for. Adeline deposed to the facts: a descent was made upon the house, the mistress was arrested and imprisoned at St.-Lazare, and the establishment was broken up.

Its mistress is the same person whom I have spoken of as having been condemned to two years in the central prison, to which she is to be transferred this morning. Will you not admit with me, Marie, that she has well merited her punishment?

As to Adeline, you will wish to know what became of her. Well, she is cash-keeper in the same store where she had sought refuge. The proprietor of the establishment, filled with admiration for the conduct of this brave young girl, bestowed upon her this honorable position. Adeline is very happy, and every month she sends one-half of the amount of her salary to her father. These little sums he lays by, in order that he may some day purchase back a portion of the grounds that were formerly attached to his villa in the Pyrenees.

Adeline made one singular condition on entering upon her new employment, which was, that she should be allowed the time requisite for occasional attendance at the public lectures given in Paris by men of science. In the assemblies which our celebrated men draw around them, one may sometimes see a young lady, simply but tastefully dressed, occupying a seat near the front, and following the speaker with the closest attention. When his eloquent voice has ceased to fill the hall, the young woman seems to awaken as from a dream, and murmurs, as she brushes away a secret tear:

"I seemed to hear the beloved voice of my father once more, reëchoing among the recesses of the Pyrenees!"

Young women, in whatever snare you may find that you have fallen—daughters, to whatever base stratagem you may be in danger of becoming victims—remember Adeline! Arm yourselves with courage in behalf of your honor, and defend yourselves!

THE DEPARTMENT OF CORRECTION.

The correctional department forms the third section of St.-Lazare, and is, so to say, a prison within a prison. Its young inmates are entirely separated from the inmates of the other sections, and have no portion of the establishment in common with them, except the court and the chapel, as they have their own shops, dormitories, and refectory. The portion of the building occupied by this department is the left wing, looking out upon the first court. Interiorly it is arranged in two divisions, "*La Correction Paternelle*," and "*La Correction Duval.*" In the department of paternal correction there are none confined but young girls, placed there by their own families, and who generally remain until they are twenty-one years of age. Their number varies from fifty to eighty. The "*Duval Correction*," so called from the name of the chief of police, who was its founder, is composed of young girls arrested by the police. At most, the number does not exceed twenty, and sometimes they are confined for only a short time.

These young girls are very difficult to manage, and give more trouble to the religious than any other class. They sleep in dormitories, divided into cells two yards square, and are entirely isolated from one another; but this does not prevent their indulging in a whispered conversation, by means of a wire lattice inserted in the wall at the foot of the bed, which, perhaps, will be replaced hereafter by glass, made to move at will. Each cell contains only a small bed and a stool. A door opens upon the long corridor on which the cells are situated. At the side of each cell-door may be seen a board, upon which are deposited a vessel of water and a napkin. Much has been said against the system of solitary confinement, and perhaps with reason; it is something dreadful for young people to live alone: however, it is but just to say that these young girls would gain nothing at all, in point of morality, by living in unrestrained association.

October 1*st.*

On leaving the "*Correction*," I returned through the corridor of the "*Pistoles*," and stopped before the cell of Clemence. I had neglected to visit her for some time, and now I found her cell empty: she had left St.-Lazare.

Marie, we have one inmate condemned to death, which is of very rare occurrence here; she was sentenced yesterday. Immediately afterward, she was brought from the "*Palais de Justice*" in a prison-van, and in such a condition of weakness that she had to be carried into the prison in the arms of the assistants. She fell three times, in mounting the stairs conducting from the office to the rooms of the community. She uttered the most piercing cries, and it would have melted your heart to hear her; finally, she was conducted to a cell, where two sisters were placed to keep watch over her. They did all they could to console her, but to no effect. She was inaccessible to consolation, and remained seated all night upon her bed, with her eyes fixed, and her hands tightly clasped. The veins of her neck were extremely swollen. From time to time she raised her hand to her head, and a painful trembling affected her whole body, while from her throat escaped the most frightful rattling noise.

The sisters passed the whole night in ministering to her wants, and praying for her. I met one of the sisters this morning, and she looked very much worn from fatigue. She said to me:

"It is frightful to behold such suffering; God alone can relieve her despair; all our care has availed but little; still, we continued to pray, and she has now become somewhat more calm."

This prisoner is one who, though young, has dipped her hands in human blood, and certainly merits the sentence of death which has been pronounced upon her; one can but hope, however, that her sentence will be commuted to imprisonment for life. In our days, it is extremely rare that a woman is guillotined.

THE DUNGEONS.

The dungeons of St.-Lazare are situated on the fifth floor in the right wing, and are eight in number. The cells are small, only two or three yards square, with a window very high up. The inlaid floors are painted stone-color, and are very clean. The furniture consists only of a camp-bed—one end being slightly raised to serve for a pillow, without either hair or straw mattress, and but two covers are left for the use of the inmate. The door is fastened with a large lock, and a little opening, of about four inches in diameter, called a *juda*, is placed in the door. These cells were constructed by the present administration, within the last five or six years.

The first dungeon that was opened for my inspection was empty. I seated myself for a moment on the little camp-bed, and I must confess that it was very hard. Some picturesque inscriptions were legible upon the walls, written, most likely, with a nail or a hair-pin. One reads as follows:

"They have confined me in this dungeon because I took a frolic."

And another, as follows:

"Andielo is a good girl; she behaved badly

with her companions, but she never was wanting in respect to her superiors, and she loves the sisters."

Other inscriptions resembled Egyptian hieroglyphics, and could not be deciphered. This is the only dungeon where the walls were written upon. As to the others, when they are disfigured or soiled, they are immediately covered again with paint, and the expense is deducted from the money deposited in the treasury by the inmate on entering; but the first-named dungeon is appropriated exclusively to young girls from the department of correction, and of course they have no money to deposit.

I looked into the second dungeon, through the little opening I have spoken of, and saw the inmate in profound sleep. She was completely enveloped in the bed-covering, and appeared like one dead. I requested that she might not be wakened, but the sister who accompanied me opened the door, notwithstanding. The woman moved, and in doing so, the wooden shoe, which she had placed under her head as a support, fell to the floor; whereupon she stood up, with the covering draped around her, looking like a spectre. I did not enter.

In the third dungeon was confined a young girl but fifteen years of age. She was sitting completely motionless, with her hands enveloped in her wrapper. The religious said to me:

"This child is very bad, and we have nothing to encourage us with regard to her future. It required four of the keepers to bring her to this room, and she continued to resist until the strait-jacket was put upon her, which we kept on for two hours."

I was shown the strait-jacket. It is made of very coarse linen, and is of a shape to fit the waist, and is fastened by leather straps with iron buckles. The sleeves are very long, and have no opening at the end, but terminate in cords, with which the hands are fastened together at the back. I looked closely at this girl; she had chestnut-colored hair and brown eyes, a fair complexion, and rosy cheeks; I could not call her homely, though her forehead was low, her eyebrows were knitted, and she was constantly biting her under lip. This made her an unpleasant object to look at. How true that anger is unbecoming to the face of a woman!

In the fourth dungeon was another young girl, whom we found upon her knees on the floor; she had a book opened upon her bed, which thus answered the purpose of a desk. This young girl was graceful, and appeared very sweet, if not really stylish, in her manners; she rose up and saluted me very politely. I immediately remarked her loosely-flowing wrapper, and asked the sister the reason. She replied:

"Madame, I always remove the belts attached to the wrappers of those inmates confined in dungeons; for, when they are very wicked, it is easy for them to injure themselves with the iron buckle."

This religious is in fact not so much the custodian as the mother of the inmates. It is she who brings them their food, opens their windows to give them fresh air, and provides them with bed-covering and books. She said to me:

"I suffer greatly when I am obliged to shut up these children; they appreciate my feelings, and close their own doors, so that nothing is left for me to do but turn the key."

Meanwhile, as the young woman remained standing, I ventured to interrogate her, as follows:

"What is your name?"

"Julia."

"For what offence are you confined in this dungeon?"

"It is six months since I came to St.-Lazare, and this is the first time I have been punished in this manner. If you please, madame, I forgot myself, and became insolent; but I am willing to submit to my punishment."

I looked at the book which she held in her hand, and saw that it was the life of St. Francis Regis. Julia said to the religious:

"I have finished reading this book; I thank you very much, sister; it has given me great pleasure; it is so tiresome to have nothing to do for several days in succession."

The religious explained that those confined in the dungeons were deprived not only of work, but of the use of books from the library, therefore she lent them her own.

There was but one more dungeon occupied, in which we found a woman seated upon the floor, leaning her head on her hands. A crust of bread lay upon the side of the bed; a pitcher of water and an empty cup stood on the floor. I entered, and, as the girl looked up, I saw that her eyes were filled with tears.

"Why do you weep?" asked I.

"Because they have shut me up in St.-Lazare, and I have done nothing to merit my punishment; I am innocent."

"Indeed! all the other inmates I have met acknowledge that they have done something to deserve punishment. Moreover, why have you been confined in this dungeon?"

"I slapped the face of one of my companions."

"That is a grave offence, and does not happen very often; but what had your companion done to provoke this fault?"

"She insulted me by saying that I was convicted at the *grande justice*."

"Explain what you mean by the *grande justice*."

"In the language of St.-Lazare, the *grande justice* is the higher court; the police tribunal is called *petit justice*. When I was sent to this dungeon, I rebelled, but sister came to me, and she spoke so sweetly that, without understanding one word of what she was saying to me, I followed her; in truth, I do not know why this good little sister fascinates me: I never would have followed the officer."

I pressed the hand of the religious, who smiled and said:

"I spare these children all the punishment in my power."

I then turned toward the girl, and continued:

"What is your name?"

"Catherine."

"For what were you imprisoned in St.-Lazare?"

"I was accused of theft; I was a domestic, my mistress was difficult to please, and I intended leaving her service; they searched my linen, and found two old pieces of worn clothing belonging to my mistress, and in the corner of my chamber they also found an old umbrella for the use of the kitchen. I swear to you, madame, that I knew nothing of the clothing, or how it came where it was found: but, upon the accusation of my mistress, I was sentenced to one year's imprisonment for robbery (*vol de confiance*). My misfortune was, madame, to have changed my position in life."

"Then you have not always been a domestic?"

"No, madame."

"Why did you enter that condition?"

"It would take a long time to tell."

"That does not matter! Go on and tell us all about it."

The sister leaned against the door, the prisoner seated herself again on her heels, and I placed myself on the side of the camp-bed, while we listened to Catherine's story, which was as follows:

THE STORY OF A DOMESTIC.

"MADAME, I am a child of Paris, born in the sixth story of a house in the Faubourg de St. Martin. My mother was a washer-woman, and washed linen for a family, living at the remote end of the same quarter in which we lived. I do not remember my father, but I believe he was dead when my little sister was born. I have a brother younger than myself, which made three children in all. My mother was a strong woman, and capable of accomplishing the labor of two in earning her children's bread.

"Our only room was scantily furnished, containing but a trundle-bed, an old trunk, and some few utensils for housekeeping; but my mother kept every thing very clean, for water was always abundant with us. Mother washed our faces every morning with a napkin taken from the first package of soiled clothes brought to our room, and, by way of smoothing our hair, simply passed her hands through the tangles, and so made our toilets after her own fashion, while we smothered her with kisses. She baked the potatoes, our invariable breakfast, in the fire made to heat the water in the clothes-boiler.

"After my mother had gone to the great boat

on the St. Martin Canal, to rinse the linen, we had our frugal meal. How we played, and what plays! How we laughed, and what laughs! Sometimes we made too much noise, for which we caught now and then many a rap from a neighbor, but we parried it off as best we could, by raising our arms above our heads.

"To dry the clothes, my mother would open our window, before which was suspended a cord to hang the clothes upon, and through which the sun entered with its warm rays, and the soft breeze. A neighbor of ours had a goldfinch, which sang for us as well as a nightingale, for we were too poor to have one of our own. We were as quiet as angels while this little singer was delighting us with his warbling, but we could not see it. I often said to my brother:

"'When I grow large enough, I shall work, and will have money to buy a bird which shall sing entirely for us. Then we can see him, and we will feed him with the crumbs left from our potatoes.'

"When my mother left us to go to the boat, she installed me as guardian over the family, and warned me not to go near the fire. I was obedient, for I was the oldest, and already understood that I must take the place of my mother, in watching over my young brother and little sister. We were very lonely; for we could no longer hear the sweet song of the little goldfinch, as our mother had carefully fastened down the window before going out; but, when we got older and wiser, my mother often took us to the boat with her, bareheaded and scantily clothed; even stockings we did not have, to protect our feet from the cold. My brother often jumped astride of the banister, and slid down even to the entrance, notwithstanding my mother's strict commands that he must not indulge in such a dangerous amusement. I carried in my arms my little sister, who was almost as heavy as myself.

"My mother attached to her shoulders a basket, made to be carried on the back, filled with wet clothes, and now, every thing being ready, we would go together to the canal. Sometimes we got very wet, for the water came up to our knees, but we were never sick, or took cold. God gives every comfort to the children of the rich, and health to the children of the poor: so, no one is left in this world without some good inheritance. We were called 'the children of the river.'

"You may not believe it, madame, but the most agreeable memories of my childhood are connected with the scenes around that great boat, with their noise and outcries. The swift-running water, sparkling in the sunshine, in which we rinsed our clothes! The innocent laugh and glee of my brother and little sister, as they played around the bucket of warm water from which I was wringing the pieces my mother had given me, and which I hung upon wooden bars to dry! I grew up in this manner. My brother was then placed at school, my sister was promoted to watch the fire under the boiler, and to cook the potatoes, while I worked with my mother. Ah! the good times we had!—the hearty poundings we gave the clothes with our beetles—our joyous laughter! We were now a little better dressed too; we earned the wages of two persons, and my sister, when left to take care of the house, was no longer alone, for she was the proud possessor of a goldfinch.

"Happy years pass quickly; suffering only makes time seem long to us. One night, my poor mother lay down on her bed, never to rise again. When she was dead, the sadness of our little home, always before so gay, was dreadful! While my mother lay stretched lifeless, where she had died, we wept in quiet grief, but, when the undertaker came to prepare the body for the grave, we uttered the most despairing cries. My brother seated himself at the feet, to prevent him from carrying her away. My little sister took one corner of the winding-sheet, and wrapped it about herself, begging them to put her into the coffin with her mother. I covered my face with my hands, my soul was torn with anguish; I was indeed beside myself with grief. The neighbors, attracted by our sobs, came and took us to their rooms, while the dear departed was being carried away. When we returned, we were indeed orphans. When we beheld our little attic room empty, we were speechless in our sorrow, and the notes of the goldfinch alone were heard!

"Without saying a word, I advanced and opened the door of his cage; he flew around us, and then lighted on the bed, on the spot marked with the impress of my mother's form, and sang to us his last song. I opened the window, he extended his gayly-colored wings and left us; we followed him in space for a moment with our eyes, then he disappeared forever. My little sister whispered: 'Catherine, he has gone to join our mother.' Since then, whenever we hear a goldfinch sing, we begin to cry.

. . . .

"My orphans had to be fed, but my wages at washing did not suffice for their support. My landlady said to me, one day: 'Catherine, you must go out to service, your wages will enable you to pay for the apprenticeship of your brother and sister, and you yourself will fare better, and will have less trouble.'

"I wept at the thought of losing my liberty, but no matter. My brother was apprenticed to a good man, who furnishes his food and lodging, leaving me with only his clothes to provide. My sister went into a workshop, under the care of religious, and they will make a good workwoman of her. A place was found for me in a family where there was not much to do, but where I would receive good wages. When the time finally came for us to be separated, our grief was renewed, for we had never been parted before.

"I had to confine myself to a kitchen, and I found it very hard: I had no air, and the water was measured out to me, as water is dear in Paris; alas! I had always been accustomed to the abundance which the limpid waters of the river afforded. I was in suffering, I was awkward, I broke my mistress's china, she scolded me, and then I would cry bitterly.

"My room was in the sixth story. One night, while I was crying more than usual, an old cook who occupied the chamber next to mine, hearing me, got up and rapped at my door.

"'Ah! child, what are you crying for?' said she.

"'I am crying because I cannot do my work well, and am scolded every day.'

"'You must not cry, you must answer back.'

"'Do you think that is right?'

"'Of course, you must give these people some reason to scold, if scold they will. You are chamber-maid, are you not?'

"'No, I am only a general servant, because I do not know how to do any thing in particular.'

"'You are a novice, poor girl! you stand in need of my advice.'

"So, she came to see me every night, gave me receipts for making several new dishes, and instructed me how to make my *petits profits* in service."

Here I interrupted her:

"What do you mean by *petits profits?*"

"Madame, I mean many things: such as the commission one gets from those who furnish articles for the house, one sou on every franc's worth of outlay, the sale of the dessert remaining after dinner, and also the gains from useless articles and clothing no longer needed."

"And you accepted these gains?"

"Yes, madame, for all servants do the like."

"Very well, you are a good girl; but still you have been stealing."

She, rising upon her feet, said:

"What is that you say, madame?"

"That you have been stealing; and that you deserve to be sent to St.-Lazare."

"Impossible!"

"I tell you it is so. Did you agree with your mistress that you could receive these little profits?"

"No, madame, nor did I know about these usages when I first went out to service. But Suzon did, and she has passed all her life as a servant. She related to me also in the evenings many little histories to divert my mind after the labors of the day. In truth, she helped greatly to make me at home in my new condition."

"Your acquaintance with this woman has been very unfortunate for you, for she might have been the cause of your being sent to the central prison for several years."

"Do you tell me so, madame? But, after all, she was a very smart woman, and used to read all her mistress's letters, and knew all about their affairs. One of her mistresses would fulfil an assignation, going out under pretence of business; another used to pay for her ball-dresses out of money destined for the poor; the third represented the household expenses as double the amount they really were, in order to obtain from her husband the difference for herself; or she borrowed of her cook, to make both ends meet at the close of the month, when she was in debt to her shopkeepers.

"While Suzon was helping to manage her ladies' affairs, she was not neglectful of her own; she appropriated the cast-off dresses of her mistresses to her own use, without asking for them; when they were not worn soon enough for her purpose, she tore them while brushing them. She also kept a little knife to scrape off the enamel of her lady's boots. Madame often reproached the shoemaker, believing that it was his fault, but still the same thing continued to happen.

"Suzon has also laid up money; and she is so well off that she is about retiring from service. Perhaps she will get married, for she has taken good care of herself, and is very well preserved; her complexion is good, as she has been in the habit of using the hygienic pomades of her mistresses. Moreover, the old cook has always made a friend of every *concierge* belonging to the different families where she lived, for she was never niggardly of either her master's wood or wine; her motto is, 'People must live.'"

"Your Suzon, Catherine, deserves to be put in St.-Lazare more than you do."

"You are mistaken, madame; this woman has an excellent reputation; she is held in high esteem by her masters, and is welcomed most cordially by all shopkeepers."

"Have you followed her counsels, Catherine?"

"As much as I could."

And this, Marie, is the way the domestics of Paris are educated. I then said to the young prisoner:

"Catherine, do not cry any more, but try and support your imprisonment without complaining, for you deserve it."

She hid her face in her hands, while I continued:

"Calculate all the little sums you have retained from your mistress's expenses, and give me your word that, when you leave this prison, you will return all to her."

"I promise you, madame, to do so."

"Illicit gains will bring misfortunes to your little orphan brother and sister. Be honest, above all things, and God will bless you. The best riches of the poor is a conscience without reproach, and their highest virtue unswerving truthfulness."

The servant replied:

"Madame, what house will open its doors to me when I leave St.-Lazare?"

"Catherine, you know, now, to what one may be brought by a slight abuse of confidence, but you are less culpable than many others; and, if at any time you are without employment, come to me, and I will find a place for you."

She clasped her hands, saying:

"In the name of the children, madame, I thank you."

I left her then, and, still accompanied by the religious, I redescended the narrow stairs leading down from the dungeons.

Marie, servants have become the plague of our days. There is need of a complete reform in their regard. In the first place, too high wages are paid. The domestics of Paris are usually young peasant-girls, just from the labor of the field. What is it that attracts them to the city? It is the high prices that we pay here. It appears certain that, if we diminish the wages paid, we shall have fewer desertions from agricultural districts, where labor is really in demand.

In the second place, we leave to them the disbursement of our money, and it is consequently the general complaint that they steal. The most natural and easy way for them to rob us is to deceive us in the matter of expenditures. The ladies themselves are responsible for this want of honesty and fidelity. It should be one of the imperative duties of every lady to pay the house-bills herself, and attend to her own personal outlay; and, to carry housekeeping to its highest perfection, she should make her own bargains.

Elegant ladies no doubt will cry out against this innovation; but, if it were *the fashion*, they would be found submitting to it without murmur. When they shall have themselves selected in market fowls or fruit for their table, do you suppose their guests will dine less agreeably? We adopt so many fashions that are either unbecoming or uncomfortable, why not for once introduce one that is useful?

Is it theft to take an article from the market-basket (*faire sauter l'ause du panier*)? Yes, and justice punishes it as such, upon a simple complaint being entered by the master or mistress. Shopkeepers who pay domestics for coming to trade with them expose themselves to be punished as accomplices. The *concierge* who aids domestics in purloining provisions of any kind, or who appropriates them to her own use, renders herself liable to the same penalties.—These are points which are often not taken into consideration.

Finally, we ought to treat domestics better than we do. Why speak to them with so much *hauteur?* We should treat them with kindness and consideration, that their condition may not be made more uncomfortable than it is already. We should see that they want nothing that is necessary to them, and we should be even liberal with them. Thus, they will become attached to our service. We ought also to watch over their morals, keep them from dangerous occasions, and, above all, not allow them to frequent balls of any kind. The evil consequences arising from these gatherings are incalculable. The moment a servant puts her foot inside of a public ballroom she is on the way to ruin.

Two thousand servants, alone, enter the walls of St.-Lazare in the course of a year.

THE INFIRMARIES OF THE SECOND SECTION.

The infirmaries of the second section were built in 1825. They are the most regularly-constructed portion of St.-Lazare, and surround the last court-yard. They are of two stories, and contain sixteen large rooms, well aired, and kept with the greatest neatness. On the first floor, to the right, is a room for those affected with skin-diseases; and at the left, the "Hall of St.-Anne," occupied by old women who are not prisoners. Between the two are the bathing-rooms, the apothecary's shop, and the clothes-room of the infirmary. All these rooms are paved with large flags, as is also the corridor, the arched roof of which is supported by pillars. On the upper floor is another corridor with rooms opening upon it. The beds are all comfortable, and each room is provided with a little table and stool.

The inmates of this infirmary do not eat in the common refectory; their dinner is served out to them from the corridor on which the rooms open. Their food is more substantial than is provided to those in health. They are supplied with meat every day—either roast-beef, beefsteak, or cutlets, as the physicians may order; each has five hundred grammes (eighteen ounces) of the whitest bread daily, and a supply of wine.

Some of the prisoners, under the supervision of the sisters, aid in the care of the sick. The costume of these assistants is a gray dress, or rather wrapper, secured at the waist by a belt; unlike the other inmates, they wear a white cap. They frequent no part of the building in common with the other prisoners, except the chapel, where they occupy the tribune or gallery, at the time of the second mass. The sick are attended by two house-physicians, and by other physicians of the first eminence, from the city, who come every day at nine o'clock in the morning.

The infirmary, although its appearance is cheerful, is in reality the saddest spot in Paris; for, there are to be found the poor victims of an irregular life, with their emaciated forms, poisonous breath, and hideous sores. Would that the women of Paris, of their class, could be brought to look upon this spectacle! Would that they might even once visit this place, appropriated for their use when disease and death shall claim them for their legitimate victims! Marie, in passing through these halls I experienced feelings of unutterable sorrow and sadness; I shuddered at the spectacle presented to me.

The first floor is occupied by public women. Let us throw a veil over their past lives, and weep for these poor creatures. Scarcely one ray of hope illumines their future, so difficult is it for them to rise from the abyss into which they have fallen, even where the desire to do so exists. One of them said to me:

"Madame, at one period of my life I abhorred myself. I strove to break my chains. I walked on foot a hundred leagues to escape from Paris. I begged my food, and slept in barns. I took by-paths, that I might not meet any one who could recognize me. I desired to put the greatest space possible between myself and the scene of my disorders. I continued to go on and on, until the sea put an end to my route. Then, worn out with fatigue, I entered a little hotel to pass the night. The next day I asked the mistress of the house for work, when she told me that, if I would do servant's work, she would employ me. I fulfilled the duties of a domestic, working hard, and proving myself obedient and docile. This lasted one month, and I had begun to live a new life, until, one day, a traveller came, and said to the lady of the house:

"'Do you know who your domestic is?'

"'No; who is she?'

"'Madame, she is a public girl from Paris.'

"In the evening I was without a home. No one would believe in my repentance, and I returned to Paris to renew my old course of life, and to die at last in St.-Lazare."

Hot tears ran down the pale cheeks of the unfortunate girl. I felt such pity, that I involuntarily held out my hand to her, but she drew back in surprise, while her tears hung suspended upon her eyelashes. As I continued to hold out my hand, however, she bent over in confusion, slightly touching my fingers, and said:

"Madame, will you pardon me for daring to touch your hand?"

"Poor child!" I replied, "God pardons all; why may not honest women be compassionate to the fallen who repent?"

Marie, do not blame me. Can she, who touches wounds that she only wishes to heal, become inoculated with their poison? The rule is, in Paris, with women of this class, who wish to change their manner of life, and who make application to this effect to the authorities, that they must give evidence to the latter of possessing other means of support. They must also find some one to go security for them, and even then they remain all their lives under the surveillance of the police.

The second floor is appropriated to the *insoumises*, by which name all fallen women are designated, whose names have not been registered on the police rolls as among the women of the town. More interest attaches to the women in this category, for great good can be done among them. Out of one hundred such characters, eighty might be saved, if sufficient resources could be furnished to accomplish so happy a result.

In general, they are very young, and are not hardened in crime; they have been brought to St.-Lazare either through poverty, abandonment, perhaps vanity, or some childish misbehavior. These are the young women who are so often to be seen weeping in the chapel. Some are reclaimed by their families; others fall at the feet of the sisters and beg an asylum of refuge; but many return to their evil ways, and finish by becoming professional outcasts.

Dear Marie, all the *insoumises* of Paris are not confined in St.-Lazare. Those are equally *insoumises*, though recognized by the world as honest women, who, under the exterior of a regular life, commit crime by bringing dishonor under the conjugal roof; of this class, also, are to be reckoned those young women who deceive their mothers, and those women in the ordinary walks of life, whose virtue is in any degree purchasable.

Thoughtless creatures, beware! You are close upon a fatal declivity; do you know how all may end? You begin with a smile of coquetry, and you will perhaps finish by realizing in your persons the premature corruption of the grave! Once that this path of dalliance is entered upon, you go on, you rush forward to your fall, and at the end the winding-sheet and the bier of St.-Lazare are reached!

Marie, these lines are for your eye alone; if worldlings should read them, they would perhaps cry anathema against me, as one who aims to proscribe what they call love. Love?—say rather crime, corruption—horror! No, this is not the scope of that high and holy virtue; it is but the guilty instinct of vitiated nature. Love is a noble and mysterious chain which binds together two hearts; it is an immaterial flame which pervades the world for the renewal of generations. True love never grovels in the earth; it is a pure flower which opens to the sun!

THE DEAD-HOUSE.

After my visit to the infirmary, I said to the sister:

"What do you do with your dead?"

She answered:

"When a prisoner dies, her body is left for two hours in the bed where she expired. Then, one of the house-physicians comes to verify the cause of death, and the body is deposited in a room known by the lugubrious title of *La Cellule des Morts* (the dead-cell). This room is on the ground-floor, and is paved with stone, cold and damp. There is in it a narrow wooden bedstead, with a straw mattress, covered with a sheet; opposite it stands a statue of the Blessed Virgin, relieved against a black wall, and having over it the following inscription: "To our Lady of a good death." In one corner lies a roll of coarse gray linen; this is the winding-sheet in which the bodies are enveloped.

The female servants of the institution take charge of the bodies for burial, before doing which, they remove from them every article of clothing belonging to the establishment, and dress them once more in the clothing the deceased wore on entering St.-Lazare. After this, the winding-sheet is thrown round the remains, which are left where they are until removed to the chapel. This practice is called *mettre les mortes à refroidir*. The domestics carry the corpse thither on a common bier, and the funeral-service is read over it.

At the time appointed, the body is placed on a common bier. Descending a few steps, and passing through a large iron door, it is deposited in a narrow vestibule. The guardians then come and open a small outside door, situated almost directly opposite the amphitheatre, through which the servants pass and place the bier upon a hand-barrow. Hence it is conveyed, by the *chemin de fer de ronde*, to the chapel.

I was present at one of these gloomy ceremonies: it was in the early evening, but already quite dark; four wax candles were burning, which shed a faint, vacillating light through the deserted sanctuary, and, as the echoing steps of the servants ceased, they heavily deposited the litter before the altar-rails.

The chaplain came; respectfully raised his black velvet cap, and knelt before the altar; when he arose, his white hair, in the light of the candles, became resplendent: thus the sweet majesty of prayer appeared to preside over the gloom of death. He commenced the office in a low voice, while two kneeling sisters gave the responses. I stood concealed behind a pillar. The whole scene made the most mournful impression on me; the solitude of the dimly-lighted chapel, and the absence of friends or relations of the deceased (for no *externes* are permitted to be present on these occasions), filled me with profound sadness.

When the prayers were finished, the body was carried out, to be taken to the amphitheatre. The candles being extinguished, every one slowly and solemnly left the chapel. A vague terror overcame me, and I hastened away.

THE AMPHITHEATRE.

The amphitheatre is a small red brick building, fronting on the road which encircles St.-Lazare, and surrounded by a wall about twelve feet high. Ascending two stone steps, you find the enclosure between the wall and the building paved with asphaltum. The interior contains two apartments, in the first of which there are three stone tables, set at a slight inclination, like the slabs in the morgue. On these, the dead are deposited. In one corner stand the bier and the litter which are used to transport the bodies.

In the other room is a round cast-iron table, which is used for dissections or autopsies. The floor is paved with stone, and a gutter for carrying off water runs round the base of the walls. Two large windows, constantly open, afford ventilation.

The spot is a sad one to visit. I very soon remarked the absence of all religious emblems: there was not even a cross over the entrance. When I spoke of this circumstance, I was answered that the place was used for the dead of all religions. I also asked why a wall was built around the amphitheatre. A person present remarked in reply:

"Madame, the windows, as you perceive, are very low; probably the wall is to keep the dead from escaping."

In spite of the painful impressions I experienced, I smiled at this joke. The real reason appears to be, to cut off the view of the interior from those who might be passing outside.

The dead who are claimed by their families are given up to them immediately. The moment death steps in, man's justice is satisfied. Friends, who wish to conceal from the world that one of their family has died in St.-Lazare, can remove the body secretly, and have it transported to their home, where the funeral service is performed. Friends do not come to the amphitheatre for their dead, but to the *cellule des morts*—the dead-cell. The bodies of those, however, who are not claimed are sent to Clamart, and serve as subjects for dissection to the medical students.

Poor women! Reduced to the lowest degree of vice during their lives, they are, when dead, delivered over in the name of science to mutilation! Or, they are buried without a coffin, wrapped only in the coarse gray linen winding-sheet. The bodies of children, and of individuals of the class of *prêvenues*, who die in St.-Lazare, are not sent to Clamart, but the authorities give them a coffin, for neither class is ranked among the prisoners—*condamnêes*, properly so called.

THE VEGETABLE-VENDER.

(*La Marchande des Quatre Saisons.*)

Among the *prévenues* there is an old woman. She is small and thin, and is dressed in a few miserable rags, for the *prévenues* do not wear the St.-Lazare uniform. Her head is covered with a kerchief of indefinite hue, from beneath which a few stray locks of gray hair escape.

I encountered this old woman while passing through the corridor which leads to the cells called the *pistoles*, which I have already described to you in a letter written during the month of August last. On seeing me approach, she drew back against the wall to make place for me to pass.

I respect old age wherever I find it, and even more under the faded rags of poverty than in the gay trappings of opulence, and I stopped to salute her. As I did so, I perceived tears rolling down her furrowed cheeks, which from time to time she brushed away with the back of her labor-hardened hand. I said to her:

"*Prévenue*, you appear to be in trouble?"

"Yes, madame, to-day is Saturday, and I have just been to the parlor to see my daughter. It is so sad to be separated from her."

"What brings you, then, a prisoner to St.-Lazare?"

"I am here, madame, for assault and battery; but I expect to be acquitted."

"*You* fighting, who seem so feeble! It must have been with a child, then."

"No, madame, it was with two great, strong women; but my anger got the better of me, and I was defending my rights, too, and that gave me strength. I assure you, they will bear the marks of my fist a long time."

"They gave you great provocation, then?"

"Madame, one of them has been the cause of all my troubles. If you care to know, I will tell you how. The other—oh! the other, God forgive her, but as for me, I never will."

I took the old woman by the hand, and, passing her arm through mine, gently led her toward the anteroom leading to the sisters' private rooms. This anteroom is an apartment through which every prisoner passes on entering or leaving St.-Lazare. It is on the first floor,* immediately above a similar apartment opening on the rooms of the keepers. Its furniture consists of a large porcelain stove, a table with reading-desk on it, an oaken wardrobe, a crucifix, some chairs, and a bench. Several speaking-tubes are inserted in the walls, to afford communication with different parts of the house.

I caused the old woman to seat herself on the bench, while I took a chair, and said to her:

* *Première étage*, corresponding to the second story in America.

"Now tell me some of your troubles, and perhaps I can do something to relieve them."

She shook her head doubtingly, and replied:

"My hopes are gone, as sure as I am a *marchande des quatre saisons*, though I have nothing to say against my calling. It is a hard one, to be sure, but I am used to hardship, and am not afraid of work. Perhaps I had better tell you how I live, madame. Ever since I was twenty years old, I have been in the habit of rising at four o'clock in winter, and in summer at three. These early hours never injured my health, for, as you see, I have arrived at a pretty good old age. When I rise in the morning, I put a piece of bread in the pocket of my apron, and start off for market, to lay in my supplies for the day.

"Madame, you have never seen the great market at five o'clock in the morning? Probably not; but you ought to—it is a rare sight. There is no end to the bunches of onions and carrots, the baskets of fish, the crates filled with fowls, as if it had rained fowls; the mountains of eggs and butter, which seem to have risen out of the earth, and the apples—ah! madame, you should see the apples! In the midst of all these piles of things, the dealers are crying their goods, and the porters staggering under loads heavy enough to break an ox's back.

"The market-women are praising their stock, and their customers running down the articles, in order to buy cheaper. Sometimes this leads to disputes, and each abuses the other with a will. Occasionally a blow passes, here or there, and if it were not for fear of the inspectors" (market police) "the blow would be hard, and there would be more of them to follow.

"This is the jolliest time of the whole day, and at last, by dint of hustling and pushing, one succeeds in getting through the business of marketing. I then carry what I have bought to my little hand-cart, which is standing in a by-street. After dressing off my *charrette* with paper or with green leaves, according to the season, I arrange my stock upon it to the best advantage. Meanwhile, hunger nips one smartly, and you should see how I relish my crust.

"In short, there I am, as happy as a queen, beginning again the round that I went over the day before, and that I shall go over the day after. So, I travel over Paris, rain or shine, crying: 'Beans! beets!' *Mon Dieu!* the cabbages and leeks I have sold in my time! In fact, I would not exchange places with a princess; for it is *working*, and not the having money, that makes people happy."

While the old woman was speaking, her countenance lightened up; the lines on her forehead disappeared, and her eyes sparkled with animation. Never did a narrator of great exploits declaim with more enthusiasm or pride. I experienced an agreeable surprise. It always gives me pleasure to find one of the common people content with his or her position in life. The old lady's last words, "It is *working*, and not the having money, that makes people happy," delighted me. The reflection gave evidence of her strong good sense. Said I:

"Well and good; you put the right value on things, to be sure, and so you are contented."

The old woman hung down her head; her expression suddenly underwent a change. She replied:

"Madame, this is only the bright side, but then, night comes, and sorrow with it. I have a good daughter, who works hard, like myself, and it is a pleasure for us to meet again, but I have a husband who is not always what he should be, and there is the trouble."

In uttering these words, the old woman's feelings overcame her. The tears returned to her eyes, as she continued:

"In former days, my husband was a worthy man, a blacksmith by trade; and for many years he was regular in his habits. While I went about Paris, carrying on my trade to earn enough to keep the house a-going, he worked too, and took care of his earnings; we were happy, and we had laid by something. But, as it fell out, he one day met with one of those unfortunate creatures who never work, but who are supported by the sweat and tears of other and better women. Since this time, our happy days are over. No more comforts, no more peace, no more savings.

"In spite of my work and my daughter's, distress came, for my husband now earned nothing. At first, I did not know the true state of the case;

I thought he was drinking. Little by little, our few pieces of furniture, and our little supply of clothing, disappeared at his hands. I said to my daughter, one day:

"'We have now nothing left, but we must conceal from the neighbors that your father drinks, and that he has stripped us as he has, for they would no longer respect him, and his dishonor would reflect upon his child.'

"Then we threw ourselves into each other's arms, and wept in silence.

"Finally, my husband would beat us, to make us give up the little money we earned. This became known to the neighbors, and they pitied us. So, one day, one of them came to see me, and said:

"'Mère Lagory, I know where all your furniture and clothes have gone; you must go and give the creature a good trouncing. Yesterday she was strutting about, dressed in the Sunday clothes of your daughter, who is now not able to go to mass, for the want of a decent dress.'

"I was not long in getting the name and address of the woman she spoke of, and away I went.

"I met the creature on the threshold of her door, and recognized her soon enough, for about her shoulders she wore my wedding-shawl. Didn't I pound her with my fist, scratch her with my nails, and bite her with my teeth! She will carry the marks I gave her all the rest of her dirty life! The woman cried like a skinned cat, a thing like herself, which knows neither how to fight nor how to work.

Then, in short, for fear of the *sergent de ville*, I made off with myself.

"As I entered my house, a little heated, I brushed against a woman just going out. At first, I mistook her for a lady, for she wore a silk dress, and her bonnet was trimmed with flowers. Bah! she was a piece like the other. The first had stolen my husband, and the second had come to steal away my daughter. As I was about to salute her, my child cried to me:

"'Mother, don't salute that *chipie*.' *

"While the woman was hurrying on, my daughter, in two words, explained her errand. I ran after the creature, and found that she and the other woman lived in the same house. So, here was round number two. Didn't I get hold of her silk dress and tear it into shreds! Didn't I trample on the beautiful flowers in her bonnet! I attempted to pull her hair, besides, but it all came off together, for it was a *wig!* Then I planted a blow—bang!—right in her jaws, and out flew her fine teeth upon the ground. 'Aha!' said I to myself, 'this will make her remember me!' And what do you think? After all, they were only a piece of dentist-work! These *gourgandines*, one never knows where to take them, for there is nothing genuine about them, neither hair, nor teeth, nor heart.

"It was upon the sidewalk I gave her this overhauling. The spectators formed a ring around us, and shouted with laughter.

* Literally, chatterbox.

"Then, here comes the *sergent de ville*, and says:

"'What, Mère Lagory, is it you that is drawing all this crowd? You are breaking the peace: you must follow me.'

"I was taken to the watch-house, then brought before the prefect, and here I am, at last, at St.-Lazare."

I found it impossible to keep a serious face while listening to the account of these amusing battles. I laughed with all my heart. The old woman, during the recital, had risen from her seat on the bench; her excited gestures had caused her cap to become displaced, and it now hung over her right ear. Resting her fists akimbo upon her hips, she thus continued:

"It is true as true can be, and as sure as that you are a good lady, who is not proud toward poor people, that I am not sorry for what I did—not a bit. I was right. Now, was I not, madame?"

As soon as I was able to control my laughter, I replied:

"Perhaps you were, but you know we are never allowed to take justice into our own hands. Mère Lagory, you are a worthy woman; I expect you will be acquitted. You will then soon resume your occupations as '*la marchande des quatre saisons*,' and, when you pass through my quarter, you must not fail to pay a visit to my cook. I shall be happy to see my table furnished with vegetables from such an honest woman as yourself."

"Thank you, madame, I shall not fail to call."

. . . .

Several days passed; and I had forgotten the old vegetable dealer, as one forgets so many other things. One morning, however, as I was just finishing my breakfast, my cook entered the room in a very bad humor.

"Madame," said she, "there is an old woman in the kitchen, who insists that I must on your account accept an enormous pumpkin, which I don't know what to do with; and I can't get rid of her."

"Oh! very likely, that is Mère Lagory; bring her in."

"*Here*, madame?"

"Yes."

"But she is a market-woman."

"I know that."

Two minutes afterward, Mère Lagory, bearing a great pumpkin, entered my breakfast-room.

"Good-morning, madame, how do you do?" said she.

"Very well, and how are you? So, you are free again?"

"Yes, madame, I was acquitted; there is such a thing as justice, I warrant. So I went to my trade again; and this morning, seeing in market this fine pumpkin, I said to myself, 'I must carry this, as a present to the lady who spoke so kindly to me at the prison.' Will you please accept it, madame?"

"Very gladly, Mère Lagory. And you will take a piece of cake, and a glass of old wine with me, won't you?"

"As to the cake, no, thank you, I have had my crust already: but as to the glass of wine, that is a different affair; that is not to be slighted: good wine is like a good woman, the older it gets, the better it becomes."

So saying, she emptied her glass, smacked her lips, and wiped them with the back of her hand.

"That is better," said she, "than the *gobette* from the canteen at St.-Lazare. But it will not do to speak ill of the other, either: still, an honest woman is much in danger of liking wine too well. I have taken a good deal in my time, myself."

"How does the little daughter do, Mère Lagory?"

"O madame, since I got home again, she sings all the blessed day like a nightingale."

"Well, here is something to buy her a nice dress for Sunday."

"Very much obliged, madame; may God reward you!"

"And the husband, Mère Lagory?"

"Well, my lady, he is doing better; the poor fellow is ashamed of his conduct, and has given up his bad ways. He is working again, and hopes to buy me a new shawl."

My cook had meanwhile remained in the room, staring with astonishment.

"Justine," said I to her, "you will always buy Mère Lagory's vegetables, when she comes around, and pay the price she asks."

"Yes, madame."

"There is no danger of my overcharging such a customer as you," remarked the old woman, as she took her leave. A few moments after, she was pushing along her little cart, and crying, "Beans! beets!"

The pumpkin remained to be disposed of, and I had it cut into quarters, and distributed among my friends. All of them found it as excellent as I did; there is a savory perfume about all honest people, that communicates itself to every thing that passes through their hands.

Marie, when you return to Paris you will meet, every day, the *marchandes des quatre saisons.* When you do, call to mind Mère Lagory's sentiment: "It is *working*, and not the *having money*, that makes people happy."

THE WORK-ROOMS.

The work-rooms are ten in number, six of which are on the ground-floor. There are two each for the *filles des cours*, the *prévenues*, and the girls of the department of correction: one for each of the other classes of prisoners in St.-Lazare, viz.: those known as the *filles des cours jugées*, the *transferées*, the *petites jugées*, and the *mécaniques*.

The two work-rooms for the *prévenues* are on the first floor, near the sisters' private rooms. They are two immense halls, furnished each with a cast-iron stove, a raised platform for the sister in charge, and chairs for the prisoners. The work-rooms for the *transferées*, the *petites jugées* (those accused of minor offences), and the *filles des cours*, have benches arranged in the form of an amphitheatre, the platform occupied by the sister being in the centre. This system affords great facility for watching the inmates, but the prisoners find it extremely painful to work all day seated on a bench. (The seats have been made more comfortable since, by order of the Empress Eugénie, who directed the change after her visit to St.-Lazare in 1867.)

The work-rooms for the inmates of the department of correction are situated on the fifth floor, and are furnished with chairs. The shop for the *mécaniques* (skilled work-women) adjoins the chapel, and is supplied with about forty sewing-machines. The work executed here is of a superior kind, as there are accomplished work-women to be found among the prisoners.

All kinds of needle-work are done at St.-Lazare, from the under-clothing for prisoners, to the most elegant *trousseaux*. The work of the prisoners is let out to a contractor, who is at the expense of warming and lighting the work-rooms. He receives half the profits of the work done, the other half going to the prison operatives. A portion of the gains of the latter is distributed to them weekly, the remainder is placed to their credit and given to them on their discharge; or, should any die in prison, this amount goes into the common treasury. The girls from the department of correction have no share in this arrangement. They receive two francs gratuity, for every twenty-four francs' worth of work done by them in a month. To earn even this, they must have spent but little idle time, for the work brought to St.-Lazare is done at very moderate rates.*

The inmates are all obliged to work. Labor of some kind is indeed essential to their happiness. In the first place, it makes the period of their detention appear shorter, while idleness would aggravate their

* The authorities of St.-Lazare have fixed a tariff of prices on all the work manufactured there, but at rates not so low as to depreciate the value of similar work done by the work-women of Paris.

punishment beyond measure. Secondly, from the pay they receive they can procure, at fixed prices, wine, *café au lait*, white bread, meats, etc. It is very desirable, therefore, that they should never be without work.

It is a noteworthy fact, dear Marie, that three-fourths of the prisoners of St.-Lazare are without knowledge of a trade, or of any means of making a livelihood for themselves, many of them having been doubtless supported by a father or a husband. This support failing them, destitution followed, and then vice. The conclusion I draw from this is, that a trade or profession is a rigid necessity for every woman, if we would guard her moral interest. Still, I believe that, in the divine economy, it was not designed that woman should labor, or at least labor for a stipend. Hence, labor is always more painful to her than to man, and more difficult to obtain. At the fall of our first parents, God said to the woman: "In sorrow shalt thou bring forth children, and thou shalt be under thy husband's power." But He said to the *man:* "In the sweat of thy face shalt thou eat bread." It is *man*, therefore, that is to labor for the support of the family, while to the woman is left the care of the household.

Man abused his privileges: not content with the power that had been granted him by God over the woman, he reduced her to slavery. Meanwhile, he was sufficient to himself for all his needs, and so could take as many wives as he was able to maintain. This is still done among nations not converted to Christianity, as, for instance, among the Mussulmans. Christianity came, and restored woman to her proper rank. Her moral dignity has consequently been established and confirmed. From a slave, she has become free; whereupon, man refuses to assist her, and she is obliged to work for herself in order to live.

The man who marries expects his wife to be subservient to him, and, by the terms of the law, the wife is bound to submit to her husband—and this is just. The law also requires the man to support his wife, which is just also; but the husband does not conform to this last condition, for he seeks a wife among those only who can bring him means, or who are possessed of a business that will yield the woman a support, and may even suffice to that of a family besides. Why may we not add, that he himself sometimes depends upon her for his own support—a thing nowise honorable in a man?

Under these circumstances, the woman he marries assumes the whole penalty God has meted out to *both* man and woman, for not only is she under the dominion of her husband, and bears her children in anguish, but she eats her bread by the sweat of her brow besides. Hence, we find many women of wealth and of intelligence who refrain from entering the married state.

God forbid that I should say any thing that would discourage any woman from embracing a state which is adapted to her nature, and is a holy one besides! nor ought she to decline it, because of the abuses existing in society; and, for my own part, I prefer that a woman *should* marry, provided she can bring with her a fortune equal to her husband's, and will have nothing to ask from him except that protection which the strong owe to the weak. But, it is well to remark that, since she is now obliged to furnish a marriage portion or its equivalent, and that, whether married or single, *she must support herself*, it is imperative that she should be familiar with labor, or be able, at least, to adapt herself to it. Thus, only, can she assure herself an honorable career in life. Furthermore, by a strange anomaly, most men are not willing to support at their own expense *any* woman, unless it be one who has forgotten her dignity. I will prove what I say.

There are almost a hundred thousand abandoned women in Paris. Who supports them? Evidently, the men, for these women do not work to support themselves. Men readily spend their means on strange women, but they are not willing to do the same for a lawful wife. Nor will they marry the woman they love the best, but rather her who will bring them the largest fortune. Hence, the lack of union we witness between husband and wife; hence, the illegitimate families which grow up side by side with, and to the injury of, the legitimate ones; hence, the numbers of young women who commence their career in luxury and idleness, and finally die in St.-Lazare. The issue of these grave considerations turns, therefore, on this: Shall our women be equal to the burden of their own independent support, or shall they not? Here is the whole question—it is one of having means, or having a trade. It is, then, for the interest of man that woman should work, and he is bound to aid her in fulfilling her task in this regard.

Let us consider now what facilities exist for women in the way of work: Hand-work is that which suits them best, but the gains from it are inadequate to their support. Administrative positions are not accessible to them; no employment that the government has to give is open to them, except occasionally a position in a post-office, a telegraph office, a tobacco-factory, or in the Bureau of Stamps, and these offices are ordinarily filled by soldiers' widows, when given to any other than male employés.

Now, intelligent writers for the public journals have not scrupled to propose that women be shut out even from these employments. The rule of debarring from such positions those women who have husbands in active service already, I can appreciate; but, to refuse them to respectable single women who have no fortune of their own, and who have the qualifications required for filling them successfully—and this, for the sole reason that they are women—is, I must say, very hard. A woman who has attained her majority, and is unmarried, is, by her circumstances, her own mistress, and entitled to the full enjoyment of all her civil rights. Moreover, she helps to sustain the burdens of the state, by her contributions, direct and indirect. Then, why has she not a right to public employment? If you do not consider her capable of filling such offices (I do not speak of purely political positions), in other words, if you consider her incapable of working, be logical, at least, and do not oblige her to pay taxes.

As to the liberal professions, it is very difficult for a woman to gain access to them. Prejudices of every kind block up her way to this theatre of action. First, the common impression exists of her inferiority to the other sex; it is believed, generally, that great thoughts, bold conceptions, comprehensive deductions, new views, are beyond the range of her weaker mental organization. I think this conclusion inexact. That her talent is entirely *different* from that of man, is true; but that it is always *inferior*, I will not admit.

To succeed in the arts, feeling and imagination are indispensable. Now, it cannot be denied that women possess these faculties in much higher perfection than men do. Women may then become painters, musicians, or authors; their only difficulty is, to bring their productions before the public. Those only who are endowed with uncommon energy, and a rare talent, can succeed in this. For a woman to enter upon paths usually appropriated by men, is an enormity in the eyes of some; not only is her talent then called in question, but sometimes her reputation is assailed. Do you wonder that she shrinks from this ordeal? Be assured, Marie, a woman must possess a reputation beyond reproach, or she must stand in no fear of attacks, if she would come before the public!

We see, then, how powerful a force is prejudice: it is incapable of judging a work on its own merits, but must look at both author and work together. Now, the private life of individuals, however legitimate a place it may fill in *history*, is by no means a fair subject of discussion for *contemporaries*. When one presents a work to the public, the public is at liberty to criticise it, but not its author.

Marie, I ask only for what is just—the right of woman to labor. Would that some statesman, with whose eloquence the walls of our assemblies are already familiar, might take up this grave question! At the hands of such a man, it would receive its just development: the light of his genius would irradiate it, and its merits would become conspicuous. Such an advocate would add new laurels to those he may already have acquired, and he would become a great benefactor, not only to womankind, but to society at large.

THE ANTIQUITIES OF ST.-LAZARE.

"THE DUNGEON OF THE ELDEST."

BETWEEN work-rooms Nos. 1 and 2, of the *filles des cours*, there is a narrow, damp passage, paved with large stone slabs, and lighted at the farther end by a barred window, which looks out upon the road that encircles the premises. An old woman, a voluntary inmate, who first came to St.-Lazare fifty years ago, told me there was on one side of this passage a very ancient dungeon that still bears the name of *le cachot des aînesses*—"the dungeon of the first-born." It is said to be about one yard wide, by two and a half in length, and three in height, with a latticed iron door, and with an iron ring in the floor, to which the prisoner was secured. A religious assisted me in searching for it, but we could find no traces of it. I was assured, however, that less than ten years ago it was still in existence. Without doubt, this was a dungeon built in the middle ages.

I could not at all understand the designation *aînesses;* however, as I believe that all traditions have some definite origin, I investigated the matter, and found that, in the time of St. Vincent de Paul, sons who brought distress upon their homes by lives of debauchery were imprisoned in St.-Lazare, and especially eldest sons, and hence the word *aînesses.*

The prisoner was brought hither secretly at night, and no one outside knew what had become of him, nor was his name made known within, to any but the superior of the house. Every means possible was employed to lead him back to a regular life and to honorable conduct, and he was not returned to his friends until a complete conversion had been effected. It is probable, then, that this very dungeon was the one used for this purpose.

OTHER ANCIENT DUNGEONS AND THE IRON CAGE.

The former dungeons of St.-Lazare were on the ground floor, very near the *cellule des morts*, and alongside the bath-rooms now appropriated to the inmates of the first section. They were dark, damp, and unwholesome. The middle one was the iron cage—*la cage de fer*—which was a dungeon constructed of iron, and into which not a breath of air, nor a ray of light, could penetrate. It contained only a wooden bedstead, made in the form of a coffin. Here were confined the most insubordinate prisoners. The spot it had formerly occupied was pointed out to me.

There are now but two dungeons in a state of preservation. To gain admittance to them, one is obliged to traverse a passage, the entrance to which is by an iron door. I was not able to visit them, for the locks have become so rusted by age that no one could turn the key. All the others have been demolished, and their site is occupied by a large hall, which the nurses use to dry the children's linen in. The iron cage is still a legacy of terror to the inmates, for it was in existence but two years ago.

THE RELICS OF THE DEAD.

It was dark, and I was returning from the chapel through one of the interior corridors, when I encountered one of the female domestics, who said to me:

"Madame, do you wish me to accompany you?"

"You are very kind; I thank you, no."

"You are not afraid to walk here, then?"

"No."

"Did you know that the dead were formerly buried here?"

"Who says so?"

"I have seen remains myself. Some years ago, when the authorities of the house commenced to floor the work-rooms of the departments for the *jugées* and *transferées*, they found a large quantity of human bones."

"What did they do with them?"

"They left them where they found them."

"Are they here still?"

"Yes, madame."

"How came they here originally?"

"Some think that this part of the house was built upon a cemetery, and that is the most probable opinion. Others suppose the bones to be the remains of those who died in St.-Lazare during the Revolution."

I made a sign of the cross, and walked on tiptoe over this place of the dead.

The next day I questioned a religious upon the subject, and she replied:

"Yes, madame, there are a great many skeletons under the workshops of the *jugées*, and on the site of the first court-yard. One day, when an old man and a younger one were at work paving, I saw several skulls dug out of the ground, evidently those of young persons, for the teeth were still sound and brilliantly white. Whereupon, the old man did not dare to disturb the earth, and continued his work without digging deeper than was really necessary. I was told, also, that medals and other religious objects have been found, but none were shown me."

THE ANGEL OF ST.-LAZARE.—A LEGEND.

Already, in 1810, St.-Lazare was a prison for women, who were either persons of bad repute, criminals, or young girls placed for correction. One day the police arrested and brought to St.-Lazare a girl who was not yet fifteen years of age, but who had become very wicked. She was placed in the smallest cell in the establishment—the cell that had formerly been occupied by St. Vincent de Paul. Madeline, when left alone, wept for a long time, and could not sleep for fear. She could see from her bed the lamp of the sanctuary and the reflection that it cast upon the windows in the chapel; but her heart uttered no prayer, for God was a stranger to her soul. The great clock struck midnight. The light in the church became more brilliant; little by little, it advanced toward her, until her cell was aglow with radiance, in the midst of which a celestial form appeared and approached the bed where the girl lay. It was an angel with great extended wings, surrounded by a transparent cloud, but the face was veiled. The figure took Madeline by the hand, and said to her:

"Arise, child, for this place is holy; thou art not pure, and must not inhabit it."

The girl tremblingly wrapped her garments around her, and followed. The spirit carried Madeline through space; and, while they floated over St.-Lazare, the night of ages seemed to revolve before them.

The present building disappeared, and in its place arose the walls of an ancient monastery. All around, the fields were covered with a luxuriant vegetation. The galleries were thronged by religious, who were proceeding to the chapel to chant the evening office of the church. Others carried upon their shoulders implements of husbandry; while still others bore parchment-rolls under their arms. A crowd of poor awaited alms at the gate.

The generation that appeared before them was one long since passed away.

Suddenly, a swift wind blew from the north, bringing with it a horde of ferocious barbarians, who with their axes levelled to the ground the fruit-laden trees, burned the harvest-stores, and invaded the monastery. The poor fled, uttering cries of distress; with eyes raised to heaven, the religious awaited death upon their knees. The convent was pillaged, and the precious parchments were dispersed. The Normans seized the riches of the monastery, which had constituted the wealth of the poor, razed the walls, and then fled in haste from the scene. The monastery was an immense ruin.

Centuries roll by, and on the site of the ruined monastery huts were erected, where persons covered with hideous sores took refuge. Other monks replaced the first, and cared for the abandoned sufferers. Toward the east, the noise of combat was heard. After each holy war, new cabins were raised to shelter the lepers arriving from the country of the sun, and who had been driven out of Paris.

In the revolution of years, still, lepers continued to be brought to the same spot, but at last the cabins were removed, and in their place another monastery was constructed, and Madeline saw some of the buildings raised which still exist. A society of poor priests established themselves here, and occupied the cells that the criminals now inhabit.

One, the most humble of all, dwelt in the cell where Madeline had been placed. When night came, he prostrated himself upon the ground and prayed. His prayer was like a brilliant flame which rose from earth to heaven. The celestial gates opened before the young girl, and displayed the seraphim gathering the rays of this flame into golden censers, which they swung before the throne of God. The brilliant light which issued thence made Madeline close her eyes, and the thought of her impure life caused her to hide herself, blushing, under the wings of her angel-conductor. Then the spirit said to her:

"I am the angel of St.-Lazare. The Creator has charged me to watch over its welfare. I come every night to the cell of St. Vincent de Paul, to gather up the tears and supplications of those who have visited that holy place. The walls of that cell have been consecrated to prayer, and one single devout aspiration hence, suffices to render the sinner acceptable to Almighty God."

The scenes of the past continued to revolve before them. Companies of missionaries went forth from St.-Lazare, to preach the gospel of peace to the peasantry, or to break the bonds of the Christian slaves among the Mussulmen. Here, too, young Levites were consecrated to the sanctuary. Every sorrow found alleviation at St.-Lazare, every misfortune assistance, every despairing soul consolation, until the angry wind of violence blew upon it for the second time.

Wicked passions were at work in the heart of France; the foundations of the throne were sapped, and it tottered; the columns of the sanctuary were shaken, and the altar trembled to its base. There was heard a violent knocking at the gates of St.-Lazare; in another instant, a frenzied multitude rushed into the convent. A scene of horror and dismay followed; the cells were pillaged, the religious driven out, the libraries delivered to the flames; the cellars were invaded, and men, drunk with excess of every kind, cut each other's throats in the darkness, while the flow of human blood became commingled with that of the wasted wine.

Death spread its sombre wings over the scene, and the angel of St.-Lazare again wept over ruins. At this spectacle, Madeline, shuddering with terror, hid her pallid face in her hands. Soon, the buildings left standing were filled with victims of every age, of both sexes, and of every rank in life, the echoes of whose sighs, tears, and prayers, resounded through the prisons.

A mournful silence followed; the angel descended and placed Madeline on her feet again within the walls of St.-Lazare. The sounds of pillage and disorder had ceased, the prisoners of the Revolution had already laid their heads upon the scaffold. Now, guilty women overtaken by justice dwelt here, and this once holy asylum, the witness to many outrages and murders, has finally become an abode of expiation. The prisoners were locked in slumber, and darkness reigned, while Madeline and the angel traversed the deserted halls.

The celestial visitor cast a radiance upon every

object in his path; he scarcely touched the ground, as he passed, and the hand of the young girl, which he kept in his own, seemed to be the only link that bound him to earth. He passed by the *Cape-cou*, and the shadows of the dead appeared, to salute him. An abrupt stairway was passed, and from the depths below, now filled up, arose plaintive voices, while mournful shadows glided through the darkness.

Madeline and the angel entered the refectory. The Lazarist fathers sat at the table, and silently ate an invisible bread. A religious was standing up, reading mysterious words from a book without characters, though distinct sounds fell from his transparent lips. When the voice ceased to be heard, the Lazarists disappeared in the darkness. In an underground room communicating with the refectory, were arranged with care the prisoners of the community. A lay-brother was asleep upon the bags of wheat. The angel touched him with the tip of his wing, and he woke lamenting. The sacks opened and were empty.

In the street now called "*La Ferme St.-Lazare*," there was a long procession of lepers, who had returned to visit the place where their little cabins once stood. Madeline and the angel paused at the entrance to the chapel. Celestial spirits lay prostrate and adoring within the sanctuary; the nave was filled with young Levites; the shade of Bossuet occupied the pulpit. His eloquent voice was full of the solemn majesty of the tomb, that earthly passage through which eternity is entered. The sounds which escaped the lips of the holy shade did not reach the ear of the young girl, and the angel, seeing she was troubled, hurriedly passed on. Entering the corridor on the ground-floor, now occupied by the *filles des cours* as workshops, they heard suppressed groans. In a narrow passage, there was a dungeon, where, writhing in suffering and remorse, a young man was confined. The angel shed some rays of light upon the prisoner, and, listening to his faint ravings, said to Madeline:

"After this manner in former times were chastisements inflicted upon those who had broken divine and human laws, in order that criminals might thus be forced to expiate their guilt. In these days, the guilty are left alone to remorse of conscience—there is freedom of repentance, all tortures are suppressed. May the guilty not await only the punishments of divine justice!"

They enter the first court-yard, and a multitude of phantoms dressed in white disappear beneath the pavement. The approach of day begins to throw an uncertain light upon the eastern horizon. The angel points out to the young girl a stone upon which a mysterious figure is engraved, and says to her:

"Your fate is connected with this stone. To-night when all is darkness, quit your cell, come hither and raise this stone; you will find under it a little silver cross, which shall be a safeguard for you. This is a place of rest, but do not fear to walk over the bones of the dead. If you wish to leave the paths of sin, an act of courage is needed, and if you dare not come through the darkness amid these wandering shades, your life will end as soon as this stone is touched. You shall be guilty and miserable, and you will die in this prison."

At these words, the girl fell upon her knees, and the celestial voice spoke once more:

"Madeline, remember the angel of St.-Lazare!"

She raised her eyes, and saw that the heavenly messenger no longer touched the ground with his feet. The veil which had concealed his face was withdrawn, and the girl was dazzled with his immortal beauty. The tints of morning were already visible, and the angel enveloped himself in the gathered rays, and disappeared.

Madeline remounted the stairs, and entered the cell of St.-Vincent de Paul. She was seized with a violent fever, and was not able the next day to leave her bed. An attendant carried her to the infirmary, and the cell of St.-Vincent de Paul was again left empty. The girl did not forget her angelic visitor, and she carefully kept the secret of the vision. She could never look upon the mysterious stone without a shudder, nor could she ever summon sufficient courage to come by night and raise it. She left the prison, renewed her vicious courses, and was several times returned to St.-Lazare. The stone still remained undisturbed.

In the course of years, Madeline returned to St.-Lazare for the last time, and her first thought was of the mysterious stone, but when her eyes rested upon it she was struck mute with terror. The court-yard was being repaved, and the stone was turned over! The words of the angel flashed through her mind. The moment the laborers had quit work, she came and scraped away the earth a few inches below the surface. She found a skull, and a little cross, with a rusty chain; she rubbed the cross upon her woollen prison-dress until it shone, and revealed the lustre of silver.

Madeline threw herself upon her knees, and invoked the angel of St.-Lazare. He came not again, but the guilty creature felt that the hand hitherto so merciful was now weighing in vengeance upon her. She doubted not that her last hour was come. The sins of her whole life arose before her, a cold sweat stood upon her forehead, and she was unable to rise. A sister, crossing the court-yard in order to go into the community-rooms, perceived her. The lineaments of her face were distorted, she was dying! Assistance came quickly, and she was transported to the infirmary. She related this history to the infirmarian, who repeated it to me with her own lips.

When the great clock struck the hour of midnight, the prisoner raised herself up in her bed of pain and cried:

"See, the angel of St.-Lazare is returning!"

At this moment, a religious was passing through the room, to whom she said:

"Sister, run to the chapel of St.-Vincent de Paul, and recite a prayer for me, and the angel will carry it up with those that the seraphim present to God, from their golden censers."

The sister believed the patient delirious, but went to say the prayer, and returned with the priest, who reconciled the dying woman with her God. When the first rays of dawn appeared, her eyes, inundated with tears, closed forever. She died at the hour that the angel had left her, on his first visit.

The prayer of the sister, united to that of St.-Vincent de Paul, had been the means of saving Madeline, and the angel of St.-Lazare carried her soul to heaven.

The same heavenly visitant returns nightly to the prison. For you, poor prisoners who dwell in it, may he warn you of the moment for repentance! May the angel of St.-Lazare bear you to God enfolded in his wings!

DUNGEONS OF PERPETUAL IMPRISONMENT.

The same prisoner who had shown me the dungeon of the "Ainesses" said to me:

"Madame, since you so love to see old things, you must visit the *oubliettes*."

"You have the *oubliettes* in St.-Lazare?"

"Yes, madame."

"Where are they placed?"

"I do not know precisely, but I will inquire."

Upon which, another prisoner was called, whom we proceeded to question.

"Do you know where the *oubliettes* can be found?"

"Yes, madame."

"Well, where are they?"

"They extend under the whole house; and it is believed that subterranean passages or vaults reach as far even as St.-Denis."

"Who says that?"

"Everybody says so."

"Oh! that is equivalent to saying nobody believes it. But do you know where the entrance to these vaults may be found?"

"I do not know; wait a moment till I return."

In five minutes she was back, and bade us follow

her. Our course led to the bathing-rooms of the second section. In front of an oven, which served to heat the water in a large copper boiler, was to be seen a wooden trap-door, more than a yard square, which, being raised, exposed to view nothing but a deep, dark hole.

Lantern in hand, and relieved of my cloak and bonnet, I prepared to enter the vault. The mistress of the baths said to me:

"Madame, do you intend to go down into that place?"

"Yes. I wish to see for myself what these dungeons are like."

Near by stood a prisoner, who in a frightened manner caught hold of my skirt, saying:

"Don't do that, madame."

"Why?"

"Who knows but there may be a deep precipice underneath?"

I smiled at her fears, and replied:

"Very well, we shall see."

A religious, more courageous than myself, took the light, and was about to precede me, when the mistress of the baths suggested:

"Madame, your shoes are very light; it is damp down there, you will get your feet wet; will you permit me to bring you a pair of *sabots* (wooden shoes worn by the peasants of France)?"

"Yes;" and a pair belonging to one of the inmates was immediately produced; but not being accustomed to wear this kind of shoe, and finding the steps very narrow, I relieved myself of them. We descended into the first vault. Venomous reptiles covered the walls; glutinous, shiny stalactites hung from the ceiling, and my feet sank into a slimy mud. In making the tour of the vault, we discovered an opening, and resolutely entered it, finding another vault built in the form of a cross, through which the water-pipes passed. We sounded the walls, which had not an ancient appearance, and could not find the slightest trace of a subterranean passage. These walls seem to have been constructed simply as a foundation to the infirmary. We remounted the difficult staircase; not, however, without brushing against a few lizards. When we found ourselves once more in the cheerful light, we breathed the pure air with new pleasure. We were not a little disconcerted, however, to find our garments covered with frightened crickets and other insects. I said to the mistress of the baths:

"Those vaults below are not the *oubliettes.*"

She replied:

"I know very well they are not; but the sick, when they are unmanageable, are made to believe that they are, in order to terrify them into quiet; the most unreasonable among them suddenly becomes docile when threatened to be let down into the *oubliettes.*"

Notwithstanding, I could not banish from my mind the belief that these dungeons really existed, and I asked myself how it was possible otherwise to account for an idea so generally entertained.

One day a circumstance occurred which excited my curiosity, and from which I hoped light would break upon the subject. I was standing before my window, which was open, and saw two men in blouses cross the "court of liberty." The unoccupied part of the first court is so called because the prisoners never pass through this court except on their arrival, and cannot traverse it again until they are free.

One of these men led a large horse by the bridle, and the other carried a long coil of rope. One of the keepers came to open a great door in the centre of the wall, through which the men passed into the other half of the court-yard. The movements of the men perplexed me. One raised a trap-door by means of a rope and pulley. The trap-door was situated near the house, and before the *casse-cou* passage. This apparatus, with the aid of the horse, was sufficient to raise from the vaults some large casks of wine; and, by the length of the rope employed, I was able to judge of the depth of the vaults.

I began to think that, by taking advantage of this occasion, I might find some clew to the whereabouts of the mysterious cells; and, profiting by the earliest moment after the men had finished their work, I descended into the cellars, exploring my way, until I arrived at the place from which the casks had been drawn out. But, alas for my hopes! I had discovered no subterranean passage.

These cellars are immense, and extend under the entire house. In some places, doors securely fastened open into them. I have visited these cellars as often as possible, and examined the ground attentively. I found, in one of the vaults on the north side, a range of dressed stone, through the crevices of which I was able to see sufficient to establish the fact that a vacant space lay beyond. At certain places I have been stopped in my course by coming upon doors now solidly masoned up. I could also hear a low murmuring as of running water, but which may have been caused by the water in the pipes.

Be that as it may, one thing is certain—I have not yet discovered the *oubliettes.* Historians have asserted that no such cells exist at St.-Lazare, but this does not satisfy me. To make sure, I must see the soil probed, and the walls sounded. I still feel a painful impression from these sombre explorations, and often have chills since the day I first descended into the supposed *oubliettes*, but the love I bear to truth makes me resigned.

October 13th.

As I was returning from a walk in the garden, I saw a small covered wagon stop before the amphitheatre. A keeper and an auxiliary (a prisoner employed in the service of the house) carried out to it some object enveloped in a sheet of gray linen, which the two placed in the vehicle. I scanned their burden closely: it was a corpse, for the limbs were perfectly defined under the folds of the winding-sheet. The sight filled me with emotion. The gloomy vehicle was then closed, and I followed it with my eyes until the great gate upon the outer road closed upon it and concealed it from view. My prayers alone accompanied the remains of one more unfortunate creature to Clamart.

October 14th.

The autumn has come, dear Marie; the yellow leaves fall from the trees, and clouds cover the sky. The air breathes sadness; the swallows have gone, and the court they inhabited is deserted. Around me reigns the solitude of a prison. I hear nothing but the murmur of the voices of the inmates, and I am engulfed in gloomy reveries. Why does not the spring-time last always? Why must the bright sun be hidden from us, and the gay green fields turn brown and sear? Why does life pass so quickly from the flowers, and youth from woman, to return no more?

October 15th.

I am suffering, Marie, and have not left my bed to-day. I have asked for paper and pen, that I may divert my mind by writing to you. This chamber of mine has been occupied perhaps by a saint, or perhaps by a lunatic, or a leper, or a poet, or a clown, and it still bears the impress of the middle ages, in spite of its modern decorations. It is a small, irregular room, with a high ceiling, and a plain floor. It has an antique chimney-piece of black marble, and there is but one window, which is very high. It is probable that my green window-shutters replace the iron bars with which it was furnished at a not very remote period; for, when I came here, this room was expressly prepared for my use. The wall has been covered by a light-gray paper studded with bouquets of roses; it is bordered with black, garlanded with the same species of flowers. I have over my mantel a painting of the Blessed Virgin, of the Flemish school, and very near my bed a magnificent engraving after Poussin. The furniture is very simple, but looks fresh and cheerful. When my curtains are drawn, and the court-yard is shut out from sight, I might forget that I was in a prison.

Marie, my dear friend, the shadow of a great name overhangs St.-Lazare. St.-Vincent de Paul lived in this house, sanctifying it by his charity, and here he finally died. I have told you that the cell where he yielded his last breath has been converted into a chapel by the religious who now have charge of the house. I kneel there with the greatest respect; I have prayed to that great benefactor of the human race to extend, even now that he is dead, a salutary influence over those who are incarcerated within these walls.

The altar now stands upon the spot formerly occupied by the bed of the holy priest; and a worn step is shown near the window, on which he used to rest his feet during the hours he devoted to labor. In a portrait hanging in the sanctuary, and said to be a striking resemblance, he seems to live again with us. If you but knew, Marie, how soothing to the fervent soul, wrapped in silent prayer, this oratory is! Imagine the religious all assembled there! When the organ vibrates under the touch of a sister, when the blessed candles are lighted, and the smoke of incense arises before the altar, then all is poetry and perfume. My earnest hope is, that you, too, may one day come and kneel in this venerated chapel; in the mean time I shall pray there for you often.

A throng of recollections presents itself to the mind on entering St.-Lazare. More than twelve hundred persons were confined here during the Revolution, among them priests, noblemen, and poets. It was from St.-Lazare that Boucher and André Chénier went forth to the scaffold.

Between the first and second courts there is a passage that the superioress called my attention to. It is known as the *casse-cou*, or break-neck passage, and is paved with large stones, with the exception of a small space covered with boards which resound under the step of the visitor. With this spot gloomy and terrible traditions are associated. The first time I visited it, a religious said to me:

"Here, during the Reign of Terror, prisoners were assassinated."

Later, a very old woman, one of the inmates of the prison, said to me:

"Madame, these large stones have been stained with blood; on this spot prisoners were massacred during the Revolution."

In fact, such is the general opinion. It is said, also, that these boards formed a trap-door, and when the unhappy victims of popular fury desired to go into the court-yard to take the air, they were forced to cross this passage. The trap giving way beneath their feet, they were precipitated into the abyss below before an appeal for help could be made. What despair, what agony and tears, have these walls beheld! I shudder at the thought. It often seems to me that I hear groans issuing from the bowels of the earth. Sometimes the lyre of André Chénier seems to resound in my ear. I listen, and I hear the plaintive words of the young and gentle captive:

"St.-Lazare.

"L'épis naissant mûrit, de la faux respecté,
Sans crainte du pressoir, le pampre tout l'été
    Boit les doux présents de l'aurore;
Et moi, comme lui belle, et jeune comme lui,
Quoique l'heure présente ait de trouble et d'ennui,
    Je ne veux pas mourir encore.

. . . .

"O Mort, tu peux attendre! éloigne, éloigne-toi!
Va consoler les cœurs que la crainte, l'effroi,
    Le pâle désespoir dévore.
Pour moi Palès encore a des asiles verts,
Les Amours des baisers, les Muses des concerts,
    Je ne veux pas mourir encore."

Then, I seem to hear his indignant rebuke of tyrants:

"St.-Lazare.

"Mourir sans vider mon carquois!
Sans percer, sans fouler, sans pétrir dans leur fange,

Ces bourreaux barbouilleurs de lois
Ces tyrants effrontés de la France asservie,
Egorgée ! . . . O mon cher trésor,
O ma plume ! Fiel, bile, horreur, dieux de ma vie !
Par vous seuls je respire encor.
Quoi ! nul ne restera pour attendrir l'histoire
Sur tant de justes massacrès ;"
. . . .

But, above all, I feel touched by these last prophetic words from his pen:

"ST.-LAZARE, 17*th Thermidor*, 1794.

"Comme un dernier rayon, comme un dernier zéphire,
Anime la fin d'un beau jour,
Au pied de l'échafaud, j'essaie encor ma lyre
Peut-être est-ce bientôt mon tour ;
Peut-être avant que l'heure, en cercle promenée,
Ait posé sur l'émail brillant,
Dans les soixante pas où sa route est bornée,
Son pied sonore et vigilant,
Le sommeil du tombeau pressera ma paupière
Avant que de ses deux moitiés,
Ce vers, que je commence ait atteint la dernière,
Peut être en ces murs effrayés,
Le messager de mort, noir recruteur des ombres,
Escorté d'infâmes soldats,
Remplira de mon nom ces longs corridors sombres."
. . . .

"ANDRÉ CHÉNIER."

[Interrupted to go to the scaffold.]

Yes, the name of the unfortunate poet yet reverberates through "the long, gloomy corridors."

Many cries of terror or of suffering have since been heard there, but the memory still haunts the spot of him who died so young, ere yet his genius had reached its full development. If I could believe that the unrecorded thoughts which occupied his brain were still floating in their germ within the walls of his former prison, I would wish to assimilate them to myself, that I might give them utterance.

What must a man think of this passing world, when he approaches the threshold of another, in the full possession of all the faculties of his soul, and the forces of his body, for the poet met death face to face, before he had attained to the natural limit of life? Tell me, O spirit of Chénier, what I so long to know. Ordinarily, we die little by little, by the gradual advance of old age or sickness, and, when the last summons comes to separate soul and body, it finds life already a half-extinguished flame.

The prisoners cross the passage of the "*casse-cou*" several times a day; laughter is heard, where so many tears have been shed! Believe me, Marie, gayety in a prison is sadder than tears.

The first time that I heard the laughter of the prisoners, my heart stood still. That one may forget misfortune I can conceive—but *shame*, never! That one may become indifferent to poverty, is not surprising; but to *crime*, how is it possible? Still, this is what we see here: and there are prisoners who are even merry, oblivious of the disgrace that follows in the footsteps of vice.

October 16*th*.

The sun has disappeared, hazy clouds cover the horizon, and sombre thoughts oppress my soul. Woman is so impressionable! she is joyous when the sky is blue, and the birds sing; she is sad and depressed when Nature lowers her aspect. She is keenly sensible to the influences which surround her, in the atmosphere, the changing seasons, the various places she inhabits, the men and things with which she is thrown into contact. Woman is like a lute, that the least contact causes to vibrate, or an Æolian harp, that responds to the lightest breeze. She adapts herself with astonishing facility to her external surroundings; she weeps with those who weep, and rejoices with those who rejoice. You must not believe that this versatility is the result of affectation on her part; no, she follows the simple impulse of her nature.

Take a joyous young creature from the midst of a *fête*, and place her face to face with wretchedness; before her smile will have disappeared, a tear will tremble on her eyelid. Woman alone can pass from one impression to another of the most opposite character. Nature has formed her thus in order to fit her for her own peculiar destiny. Her place is in the family, and, while she shares with her husband his cares and vexations, she must smile with her children, and mingle in their sports. Woman has an admirable organization, to which justice is not always rendered, for her flexibility is generally called inconstancy.

Is woman, in truth, light or inconstant? No, she is capable of the greatest depth and concentration of feeling; her affections and her sorrows, time cannot change. All that is light and trifling in her character she owes to the education she receives, to the ideas inculcated in her mind from her earliest infancy. As the consequence of her childish treatment, frivolity must become her second nature.

October 17th.

Marie, how many women fail in their duty! It is because they do not know themselves; they forget their own value, or they never knew it. The sentiment of personal dignity is not sufficiently developed in woman: and yet, this sentiment is, when united with religion, the only solid basis for a moral education that is to develop her real dignity. It is impossible for a woman who understands and remembers her true destiny to degrade herself. Such a one may be led away for a moment, through weakness, but to sink to the lowest depth would be difficult for her.

I asked a prisoner, who had been a great criminal, by what steps she had fallen into vice. She was a very intelligent person, and appeared to have received some education. Her reply was:

"Madame, few women would dare to throw themselves away if they only knew the cost of the step. After my first fall, my better nature revolted, and I experienced such shame and despair, that I could have taken my life. A friend, one of my own sex, but an evil counsellor, who came to see me, said:

"'You are suffering; you must seek distraction, and try to forget your troubles,' and she presented me some champagne. I drank until I benumbed my senses. I did the same at every new fall, but I did not arrive at the last degree of debasement until I had stifled every noble instinct, and until, through drunkenness, I had forgotten my dignity as a woman."

This unfortunate creature was only twenty years of age. She died a few days after.

October 18th.

The wind blows fiercely around the prison today, and the sound penetrates to the secret recesses of the soul, and seems to comprise the concentrated sighs and groans of all who suffer here. Can we not distinguish in all this sad concert the griefs of woman? She endures sickness, poverty, oppression, disgrace, and abandonment, for faults in which she is but an accomplice. Young girls, wives, mothers, all have suffered, all will continue to suffer. Let us pity our sex, Marie; let us pray for them, and pour a little balm into their wounds, when opportunity presents.

October 19th.

I have come to the conclusion, dear friend, that the fate of woman depends in a great measure upon man. Those who are happy, owe their good fortunes to their husbands, or to their fathers, or to some other male member of their family. How thankful they should be to God, and how devoted to their natural protectors! The affection of a woman's heart is a source of joy to a man. She knows so well how to alleviate suffering, to dissipate sadness, and to lighten the weight of care. She knows how to change cheerfulness into joy, and render happiness more than complete. If men knew how sweet a pleasure it would bring to their own hearts to be good, to be just, and to be generous; if they knew how advantageous it would be to them to render effective protection to the women by whom they are surrounded, or to whom they are united by the ties of blood, would they speak only of their own *rights*, and of our *duties?* No; their rights may be written in the law, but our duties are written only in our hearts. If they would aim but to win our affections, there would be nothing wanting to the happiness of either side.

October 20th.

I have just returned from a ramble through several of the prison corridors. At this hour, the inmates are engaged in the workshops, and all the cells are empty. I have inspected several of the latter. The little beds were all covered alike, with a brown woollen coverlet, finished off in the neatest manner. Order and cleanliness reigned throughout. On approaching one of the cells, I heard a voice singing, in a sweet and plaintive tone, like that of a mother hushing her child to sleep. It was that of a prisoner, one who had evidently not undergone trial and sentence, for she was not yet clothed in the prison uniform. She was young and beautiful, and her dress indicated a person of the better class. She was seated on a stool before her window, with her eyes fixed upon the court-yard, but her thoughts, without doubt, were elsewhere, for she sang vague words to a monotonous air, which she timed with a slight movement of the head. I caught a side view of her face; it was pale, and her chestnut-colored hair descended in large masses upon her neck. For an instant I entertained the thought of going into the cell to speak with her, but, as my visit might not have produced a good effect, and she appeared so peaceful and resigned in her solitude, I concluded to leave her to her own thoughts.

It is now mid-day; the inmates of the department of correction are taking their recreation. At the first stroke of the "angelus" they simultaneously drop down upon their knees, in the midst of the court, while the sister on guard recites the prayers in a loud voice. It was touching to hear these young girls make the responses. For them the prison of St.-Lazare proves a boon rather than an evil. Happy will they be if, on leaving the prison, they carry with them the habits of order, of labor, and of devotion, that they have acquired while here!

October 21st.

Dear Marie, I have seen an unfortunate creature die, and so young! She was old in wickedness, but young in years. Her features were regular; she might once have been handsome, but there were no longer any traces of beauty left. Her pale face rested languidly on her pillow; her emaciated hand was scarcely perceptible, in its whiteness, upon the counterpane. Those present were on their knees, holding lighted candles in their hands, for the priest was present with the holy viaticum. All were in tears, save the dying girl.

"I am glad to die," said she, "for this life has not been to me a happy one. The days of my youth have been short and full of evil. What remorse I feel for my guilt! God will, I hope, have mercy on me. Pray for me, for I have but a moment left for repentance."

She raised herself up to receive communion, and, overcome by the exertion, fell back exhausted. An hour after, she was no more.

The next day I assisted at the mass celebrated for her repose. The prisoners carried her remains into the chapel, and, after the prayers for the dead were finished, a solitary hearse served to carry her remains to their last resting-place. Not a relative, not one friend to shed a tear on the lonely coffin, followed her to the grave! She had abandoned her family, and her family disowned her. She had bartered her youth for a few days of foolish pleasure, and those who took her beauty from her gave her nothing in exchange but disgrace. She has passed away without leaving a trace; once dead, she is utterly forgotten. Young women, watch over yourselves, prepare yourselves for a useful career, and live nobly, if you would die beloved and regretted.

October 22*d.*

There is not a being in the world who has received greater censure, and at the same time been more highly extolled than woman. I affirm that the most contradictory things may be said of her that it is possible to suggest, and reason may not be able to dispute it. The life of man runs on in an undeviating round, by which his existence and character are modelled into unity; but not so the life of woman. Her days are an alternation of the good and the evil things of life; sometimes she will be full of vigor, of health, and of sound impulses, charming in her disposition, flashing with wit and gayety, desirous and capable of accomplishing the most difficult things. At another time she will be found feeble, sick, capricious, melancholy, witless, egotistic, and incapable of the slightest effort of mind or body. There are days when the most superior woman has not one lucid idea in her mind—days when one who is ordinarily most devoted to others will forget all her obligations, and become entirely devoted to her own selfish pursuits.

But can this be said to be the true character of woman? No, no more than it can be said that, because of one stormy day, storms are the normal condition of Nature. Those who have praised her too much have only considered her good qualities in her happy moments. Those who have blamed her without measure have seen nothing but her faults in her days of gloom. To be just toward her, she must be seen in all her aspects, and be judged by all her works.

THE CHAPEL OF THE PRISON.

I HAVE already spoken, my dear friend, of St. Vincent de Paul's chapel, but I have said nothing as yet of that of the institution, although I visit it nearly every day. I choose, for this purpose, an hour when it is not frequented by others, that I may pursue my meditations undisturbed. How I love its mysterious silence at such a time, when the wooden benches are empty, and only the solitary lamp burning before the hidden Presence in the tabernacle! Nothing distracts me here, except an occasional voice from the court-yard where the prisoners are in recreation. The hours spent here are delightful in my memory.

When approached by the interior corridors, one enters through a large vestibule which served the same purpose to the old chapel, now demolished, but upon which spot the present one was built in 1828. Over the entrance, in black letters on the white wall, are these words from Scripture: "This is the house of God and the gate of heaven." On the right is the sacristy, over the door of which is the impressive inscription—"Silence, for God is near!" On entering the chapel, that which strikes the eye first is a vast tribune, supported by plain pillars. The inclosure, the same as the tribune, is entirely filled with wooden benches, painted the same color, and destined for the use of the inmates. In front of these, and separated from them by an iron railing, are six benches, varnished, and kept brightly polished, for the use of the religious.

The altar is placed very high. Ten stone steps lead to the communion-rail, and, to reach the platform of the altar, five more steps, arranged in a semicircular form, must be ascended. The high altar is of oak, and in plain style. Above it is a statue of St. Vincent de Paul. Over this, again, is a good copy from Prudhon's painting of Mary Magdalen at the foot of the cross. The face is in shadow, and only one shoulder is presented to the light. This portion of the figure, although not irreproachable as a work of art, has, nevertheless, a life-like appearance, and one seems to see the flesh shudder under the weight of Magdalen's grief, as she ought to have shuddered in the midst of the world's voluptuous *fêtes*.

Representations of this great penitent always affect me profoundly. This prisoner of penance, breathing out her life in tears and regrets, and ending her days in the depths of a frightful desert, presents fallen woman with the example she should follow, if she wishes to expiate the past. Many of the poor creatures who kneel before this picture must experience anguish and remorse like hers. How many tears have not been shed in this chapel —how many sobs heard within its walls!

Six large stained-glass windows light the chapel,

surmounted by a dome. The roof is supported by eight columns of the Tuscan order of architecture. Beside the sanctuary is a dimly-lighted oratory, dedicated to the Blessed Virgin under the title of Our Lady of Reconciliation, a favorite shrine of resort for the prisoners. In addition to the lamp which, by the care of one of the religious, is kept constantly burning before this altar, the prisoners daily bring candles. The statue of the Mother of God is so covered with rich satins and laces that only the head remains visible. This statue was found by one of the sisters in a pile of rubbish, which was first given an honorable place in the house, and afterward placed in this oratory, which was erected expressly for it.

The devotion practised by these unhappy and guilty women toward the pure and immaculate Mother is most salutary and consoling to them. At the feet of Mary, they find not only relief from present woes, but hope for the future. Sometimes they come here to pray with a heart loaded with despair, and rise from their knees full of resignation and courage, and resolving to bury in a cloister the sins and miseries of the past. Why do not the pure and honorable of our sex imitate holy Mary's clemency, and extend the hand of compassion to elevate the fallen?

The chapel can seat nearly six hundred, and, in order that all may be present at the offices of the church on days of obligation, the *prévenues* are assigned to the tribune. The behavior of the prisoners at mass, to whatever section they may belong, is admirable. I will do them the justice to say that in this they impressed me most favorably. It is proper to remark, however, that the least infraction of the rules of order and decency at such a time is severely punished. Many among them stand in awe of the chapel: they are afraid of being *converted* there. There are others who do not offer any interior resistance to the sweet spirit of prayer, nor close their ears to the paternal exhortations that are addressed to them. These return to God and to a worthy and honorable career, blessing St.-Lazare and its chapel for the remainder of their lives for having been the means of rescuing them from the paths of vice.

All religious ceremonies in the chapel are performed with splendor and solemnity. The chapel is always decorated with fresh flowers, the linens are spotless in purity, and all the ornaments are kept in the neatest order. The chaplains of St.-Lazare are men who have grown gray in the service of the sanctuary. In laboring for the spiritual interests of the prisoners, they employ a fatherly tenderness, united with an apostolic zeal. They are held in the highest respect and veneration, and the good they accomplish is very great. However, they employ no influence over the prisoners except that of prayer and exhortation, for the sacraments are not made obligatory on the inmates of St.-Lazare.

Sometimes preachers of great distinction come hither to assist the chaplains in their work of drawing souls to God, and on leaving uniformly testify to the edification they have received from the conduct of the prisoners, and to the emotion excited in them by the evident signs they see of repentance. The time has long since passed when an archbishop, of holy memory, dared not visit St.-Lazare for fear of receiving insults.

PROTESTANT WORSHIP.

All religious creeds are respected at St.-Lazare. Near the infirmary of the first section is a room exclusively for the exercise of Protestant worship. The room is small; somewhat wider than it is long. Two benches occupy one side of it, and opposite them is a platform and desk for the minister. Above this hangs a simple wooden cross. The window faces the entrance, and the room is heated by a porcelain stove. There are four tablets on the walls, on one of which is inscribed the Lord's Prayer, on another the Apostolic symbols and on the remaining two the Ten Commandments.

Lady deaconesses come every week, sometimes every day, to visit the Protestant inmates.

JEWISH WORSHIP.

Immediately opposite the Protestant chapel is that for the Israelites. I expected to find here some Hebrew inscription, or at least some verses from the Old Testament, but there was nothing to be seen except a table, a few chairs, and some books on a shelf.

October 23d.

. . . .

I am fatigued; I have overtasked my strength by writing to-day. The atmosphere is heavy, damp, and unwholesome. I feel the absence of the sun. Dear Marie, how I sigh for the blue skies and the lovely mountains of our own Provence! Can it be possible that I may never revisit it?

October 24th.

A mother's influence with a daughter is immense; not only has she imparted to her the blood that flows in her veins, and nourished her with sustenance from her own breast, but she communicates to her her own good or bad qualities, and sometimes, as we see, shares with her her own intellectual gifts.

There was a mother who had seven beautiful daughters, who were intelligent, but somewhat fond of pleasure. However, having been educated by a mother not only exemplary in her character, but industrious in her habits, they were good and industrious like her. The mother died; the daughters, no longer sustained by her salutary influence, began to neglect their domestic occupations. The home made so sweet by the mother's presence, soon became distasteful to them, till finally they abandoned it altogether, and entered upon the stage. One of them is at this time an inmate of St.-Lazare, who said to me only the other day:

"If my mother were still living, I should not have been here in prison."

Now, since this brings me to mention the stage, I may ask why it is a word synonymous with moral debasement? Who and what is an *artiste* or actress, Marie? She is a person who is ordinarily endowed with courage, energy, and intelligence. Her *rôle* is to interpret genius, and to give a living form to its creations. An actress is one entitled to consideration, because she works for a living. Why, then, is she not more respected? Why is she not received in society? It is simply because she does not appreciate her own value, and places herself in a false position; she is not satisfied to remain a worthy person, maintaining herself honorably by her profession, but she aims to lead a life of luxury, and so she adds, to the toilsome work of close study and frequent rehearsals, the wear and tear of a life of pleasure.

Let me counsel actresses of talent, to leave grand toilets and costly jewels to lorettes and courtezans. Make no effort to shine otherwise than by your own genius, and then you will not be tempted to part with your highest honor. Lead a life of regularity. Your position is a difficult one to fill, and you require a protector; it is one of constant toil, and you should seek repose in the surroundings of a home; therefore seek a suitable companion for life. Whom shall you marry? The scion of a family who will never forgive him for his *mésalliance?* One who will force you into a circle unwilling to receive you? No. Such a marriage would be as ill-advised and ill-assorted for you as for him. Your profession demands that you seek the presence of decided talent in your husband, with which, unhappily, the sons of distinguished families are rarely endowed. Marry an artist like yourself; he will not only protect you, but will cause others to regard your rights and respect your person. You have your profession by which you can distinguish yourself, and make a fortune, and, what is much more essential, you will have a home in which to be beloved. This prospect should satisfy the aspirations of the most exacting.

Marie, the French people will never consent to abandon the theatre as a place of amusement, and, if actors would lead more regular lives, their talents would be brought to a much higher degree of perfection, and, in place of seeing our favorite actresess in the midst of their stormy career fade and fall before their time, we should have those who are aiding to develop the higher and better sentiments of the people; then the *chefs d'œuvres* of art would displace the stage-tricks and unmeaning pageant of to-day. Once make our artists happy in their conjugal relations, and we may expect to behold the stage correspondingly elevated. Do you believe such a state of things to be impossible? We have actresses already who are married, and lead honorable and exemplary lives, and enjoy that preëminence in their profession which is due to their entire devotion to it. All honor to such! I trust that their noble example will be imitated by others. Whenever such as these appear upon the stage, may the public redouble its applause, as a compliment to their industry and their honorable conduct!

October 25th.

It rains, Marie, and it reminds one of that heavy, cold, eternal rain, of which Dante speaks in his "Inferno." The continued, monotonous sound, made by the drops falling upon the pavement of the court-yard, strangely impresses my mind, and prevents me from pursuing any regular train of thought. I have dropped my pen, and fallen into one of my usual dreamy reveries.

October 26th.

In the second section, appropriated entirely to females of disreputable character, there is a young girl who bartered her virtue for the sake of bread for her mother. Her history is truly a sad one. Her mother was ill, and, although totally unable to procure the remedies she needed, shrunk from the idea of going to the hospital. The pittance her daughter earned by working all day and a part of thenight, by the dim light of a smoky lamp, was exhausted; and their poor garret was without clothing or fire, nor was there even a spoonful of broth for the sick mother.

Wearied and desperate, the girl went out to seek aid. She returned, sadder, paler, and more desperate than before, but she brought a piece of gold! The mother always remained in ignorance of the means her child employed, to meet the expenses of their humble home, or in what manner their every want was now supplied; and to-day the girl is an inmate of St.-Lazare. With suppressed sobs, she said to me only yesterday:

"O madame, how wretched I am! If my mother knew the whole truth, she would die with shame. And now see what I suffer for my devotion to her!"

I replied that duty to parents did not require us to commit a crime, nor transgress in the least the limits of virtue.

A woman's most precious treasure is not life, but honor. Death, with honor unstained, is preferable to a life of shame. But, my dear friend, if there are daughters who sell their virtue for the sake of their parents, there are also mothers who sell their children for a selfish gain to themselves. A crime more horrible than this it is impossible for a woman to commit. For its punishment all the resources of human legislation are inadequate, and only divine justice can measure out a penalty at all proportioned to its deserts.

October 27th.

A young mother has just arrived. The keeper held her infant while she descended from the van, and carried it with the greatest care. As she entered the prison-door, the mother affectionately clasped her child in her arms, and with moistened eyes thanked the kind keeper.

THE NURSERY HALL.

One of the most touching sights to be seen in the prison are the "*Salles des Nourrices*," for the reception of prisoners with infants. Yes, Marie, strange as it may seem, there are many such mothers sent here. I often see the interesting little creatures, seeking the sunshine that makes its way through the bars which protect the windows, and shut out from air and liberty to expiate the mothers' fault. With delicate forethought, the authorities have appropriated to the nursing-mothers two apartments looking toward the south, into which the sun shines a good part of the day, so that the children may bask in its healthful beams.

These apartments contain from twenty to twenty-five beds each, those of the children being placed at the foot of the mothers'. There are from fifty to sixty children, for some of the mothers have several each. These little ones are allowed to remain at St.-Lazare until they are three years old, when they are removed to the depot. They are well cared for; the establishment spends twelve hundred francs a year for milk to make their porridge. One day, in crossing the halls, I saw a sister weighing out the beautiful flour of which the mothers made their food. The mothers have the same fare that is assigned to the inmates of the infirmary.

One of the rooms, called *La Salle des Transferées*, is appropriated to those who have been sentenced to the central prison, but who are permitted to remain in St.-Lazare, on account of their little children. The other contains those who are imprisoned for only a short term. Marie, I beg of you to devote your leisure moments to making clothes for these little ones. So long as the mothers remain in prison, their linen is supplied by the house, but, on leaving it, this linen is given up, and they are often destitute of means to procure more. I know this to be so, from a circumstance I witnessed. I met a mother just as she was leaving the prison, who seemed very happy, and who carried in her arms a remarkably fine child. But the latter had hardly any clothing on, and its pretty little feet were bare, being only wrapped around by a corner of the mother's apron. Will you not send me something for the poor little things ?

Notwithstanding, Marie, that vice and crime abound here, we meet occasionally with striking examples of virtue and self-devotion. The little history I am about to relate will illustrate this.

THE TWO FRIENDS.

Two young seamstresses were engaged at work in the same shop. One was an orphan, and had no relatives except grandparents, who lived in a distant province. She herself dwelt alone in her garret in the *Marais*. Aglaé, for that was the orphan's name, worked all the week for her employer, and Sunday being the only day she had for herself, she put to rights in the morning her little chamber, went to mass, and afterward took a long walk in the open air. She was happy, notwithstanding her isolation. Her toilet was modest, her wages were sufficient for all her simple wants, and she envied no one. She had never set foot in a ballroom, that place where so many of the poor work-women of Paris have been lost. Her natural integrity of character, and, above all, the religious principles that her mother had instilled into her heart, preserved her from exposing herself to such dangers.

Sophia, her companion, belonged to an industrious family, who took a just pride in their good name. Her mother, though at times abrupt in her manner, was an honest woman, a good wife, and a good mother. She divided her time between her daily labor and the care of her children, and kept good order in her household.

One winter, Aglaé fell sick, and Sophia and her mother attended her with the greatest care, as worthy people of their class are wont to do for one another. The orphan recovered, and vowed lasting friendship to Sophia, and unlimited gratitude to Sophia's good mother.

Sophia was in her eighteenth year. She was beautiful, and she knew it. The consequence was, that she began to show a love for dress, and if her mother had not rigidly prohibited every kind of vain display, she would have expended her wages in ornaments for her person. Aglaé felt great solicitude for her friend on this account, and often remarked to her that simplicity in dress was the most becoming attire for a young girl, and above all for a humble seamstress like herself. Sophia incredulously shook her head.

Now, there was employed in the same shop with the two friends, a young person of a gay disposition, and whose conduct was not above suspicion. This girl had quite captivated Sophia. She was very fluent on the subject of dress, fashions, etc., and finally talked so much about balls, that Sophia was seized with a feverish desire of going to one, even if it were but for once. Julia removed every difficulty by assuring her that no one would know any thing about it. But, to go to a ball, one must have a suitable outfit, which Sophia did not possess. This was a great obstacle, which Julia, however, was not long in disposing of. She took down a box from her employer's shelf, filled with muslins, Valenciennes laces, and flowers, saying:

"See, what a lovely toilet you can make of these!"

Sophia's eyes sparkled with delight.

"Very well," she hurriedly answered. "I will use them to-day, and replace them to-morrow."

Accordingly, a toilet was improvised, and they went to the ball. Two hours of frivolity were spent here, and Sophia's vanity was satisfied. But, how bitter was the return! Clearly it was quite impossible for her to show herself in her mother's rooms, with that tell-tale finery on. So, after great perplexity, she concluded to go to Aglaé. The latter had been quite sad at the thought of her friend's having left her alone so long, and so, when Sophia had made her appearance, she joyfully embraced her. She immediately perceived that Sophia was troubled, but the latter volunteered no explanation, and returned to her mother's apartments, after leaving with Aglaé, without comment, the flowers and the white dress she had worn. The orphan passed a restless night, for she had a vague suspicion of the truth, and she wept many tears for her friend.

The next morning, as Aglaé was preparing to return to her shop, a violent rap was heard at the door. It was Sophia, who entered pale with alarm, and her dress in disorder. Throwing her arms around her friend, and clasping her tightly, she exclaimed:

"Save me! Oh, my poor mother, she will die with grief! I am ruined; they have come to arrest me. That toilet—I stole it. The police have been notified, and they are in pursuit of me."

At this moment another rap was heard, and Aglaé went to the door. There stood the policeman. The orphan grew more pale than the guilty one herself; her strength failed her, and she clung to her little bed that she might not fall to the floor.

"What do you wish, sir?" said she.

"I have come for a young girl who has taken refuge here with you, Sophia R——."

"What do you want with her?"

"She is accused of theft, and I am come in the name of the law to arrest her. We were at her house, but she had left; and, from the direction given by the porter, we have traced her here. She is with you?"

"Yes, but she is innocent."

"That is not your affair, miss. Search is to be made at her house for the flowers and lace that she has purloined from her employer."

"That is unnecessary," said Aglaé. "However guilty I may be, I cannot consent that another should also be accused."

Whereupon she opened her wardrobe, and the policeman beheld the articles that had been described to him as stolen.

"I am the thief," said she, resolutely, "and I am ready to follow you."

Sophia, lost in astonishment, had not uttered one

word; she could not have conceived that her friend should employ so sublime a means of saving her. But, as Aglaé was about leaving her chamber to follow the officer, the unfortunate girl bounded toward her to beg and protest that she should not make the sacrifice. Aglaé, however, checked her, and said:

"I am alone, but you have to think of your poor mother!"

Then, placing her finger to her lips, she disappeared. Sophia wrung her hands in despair, and, falling on her knees, she cried:

"What a wretch I am! My God, my God, have pity on me!"

Aglaé was condemned to six months' imprisonment, and is now an inmate of St.-Lazare. Dear Marie, is not such devotion admirable? When, amid examples of so much vice, we meet with generosity like this, we become reconciled with human nature. The young orphan bears her imprisonment nobly. As to Sophia, she is cured entirely of her love of display, and will never again put her foot inside of a public ballroom.

October 29th.

I can see, from where I am sitting, a prisoner sitting in her cell, and occupied in braiding her hair. There are no mirrors permitted in the cells, as you can readily suppose, and this pretty young creature is plaiting her magnificent black hair with a pane of glass for her mirror. Unfortunate child! Shut up in a prison, she yet allows her besetting sin to control her! Do not ask me what she has done to bring her to this place; her vanity, without doubt, brought her here.

How many women are lost through the love of dress alone! Luxurious living, together with the ambition of attracting admiration and attention, constitutes the crying evil of the age. The desire to please, Marie, is a natural sentiment that God has implanted in the female heart; it is a continual homage rendered to man, though it is from man, paradoxical as it may appear, that our severest rebukes for this propensity emanate. At the same time, it is but just to say that it is the excess only of this quality which is blameworthy.

Indeed, it is difficult to comprehend why our sex should take so much pains to captivate the other. Women would succeed much better in their object by maintaining their dignity. Let them preserve their beauty, and turn to account the advantages they may have received from Nature, if they will; I find no harm in this, provided the influence they aim to exert be of a salutary character, and that they make use of their attractions only to make men love virtue more. Let the wife adorn herself for her husband's sake, that she may make home more attractive to him, but let her not use the same means to win the admiration of his friend. There is one fault for which married women generally are worthy of reproof, and it is that they indulge themselves in too great negligence in dress at home, and make too expensive and elaborate toilets for the benefit of strangers. What folly, to endeavor to please those we only casually meet, and possibly may never see again, while we neglect to make ourselves agreeable to those who hold our happiness in their keeping!

November 1st.

Women are naturally jealous, and this trait often causes them to commit the most treacherous acts, and sometimes even the most odious crimes. I would rather arouse the hatred of ten men, than the jealousy of one woman. A woman's stronghold is the heart, and, if there be any interference with the object of her affection, her entire happiness is at stake. How adroit and malicious will she then be in the use of means to revenge herself! Dear Marie, you have wit, feeling, and beauty, but, if you should ever be tempted to play the coquette, beware of *the women!*

November 4th.

There is an improvement greatly needed in the interior arrangements of St.-Lazare, especially in that which requires each cell to contain several beds —an arrangement the inconvenience of which struck me forcibly on my first visit to this prison. First, it makes the care of the prisoners too difficult; and, secondly, the air becomes very foul in these small apartments. All the division walls between the cells should be removed, and one large, well-ventilated dormitory constructed, where a few domestics could exercise all needed vigilance. When I gave my opinion to this effect, I was told that the building was not sufficiently strong to bear such a change. However, in the infirmary of the second section this has been done already, and pillars take the place of the walls in supporting the ceiling.

St.-Lazare was not originally intended for a prison, and the cells are the same that were once occupied by the Lazarist Fathers, before the Revolution. Another inconvenience strikes me as very serious. I cannot comprehend why women under arrest before trial (*prévenues*) should be sent to a *prison* like St.-Lazare. Among them must necessarily be many innocent persons, and it is not just to bring such in contact with the guilty. It must not be forgotten that the morals and the reputation of a woman are like a delicate flower—once tarnished, they remain so forever.

When the prisoners are discharged at the end of their term, the greater part find themselves, on quitting St.-Lazare, without a home, and even in want of indispensable clothing; it is very difficult for them, moreover, to obtain work or employment, and they are consequently greatly exposed to become the prey of the "*marcheuse*," who prowl around the police quarters to entice these unfortunate creatures into houses of vice.

A young girl, twenty-one years of age, very amiable and pretty, was condemned, for some trifling fault, to a month in St.-Lazare; she had no acquaintances in Paris, and was greatly distressed at the thought of what would become of her when she regained her liberty. A lady friend of mine consented, on my recommendation, to employ her in the capacity of chambermaid. The poor creature shed tears of joy at the announcement. She left the prison, and the lady expected her day by day, until a week passed, but she never came. I am convinced that, if I were to inquire at the office of the prefect of police, I should find her name registered as an inmate of some house of ill-repute. She has undoubtedly fallen into the snare set for her by some emissary of these abodes. These creatures receive five francs for every new subject they bring to a den of infamy. Such prisoners as are converted from their evil courses, and decide to withdraw from the world, find immediate refuge in some one of the religious houses founded by the sisters of Marie-Joseph, established in various parts of the country, for the reception of penitents who give hopeful signs of perseverance. From fifty to sixty are thus received yearly from the various sections of St.-Lazare. However, many young women, who really desire to lead good lives for the future, have no vocation to become religious, consequently some secular institution is needed as an asylum for this class. An industrial establishment should be provided, where they may at once find shelter and work, until such time as suitable employment could be procured for them in Paris.*

To realize this desirable object, a house furnished in the plainest manner is all that would be needed, for the labor of the inmates would be sufficient to support it.

Marie, there are great resources for charitable objects in Paris; I put my trust in God, and I appeal to the sympathies of my sex, that this succor be not long withheld, and that thus a great number of young women may be rescued, who must otherwise be lost.

November 12th, four o'clock in the evening.

It is Sunday: the weather is very lovely for the season, and the western sky is radiant with golden tints. The court-yard is crowded with the prisoners, and an indefinite murmur of voices is heard. Great numbers of sparrows are sporting among the branches of the partially-denuded trees, and their merry song is heard above the voices of the prisoners. The workshops are closed, the prisoners have attended divine service, and they are now left to recreate themselves for the remainder of the day, and they know well how to appreciate the time. God has designed this day as a day of rest for all the children of men.

* See Appendix, where particulars are given of an institution of the kind, since undertaken.

LIFE WITH A FREE REIN;

OR, RECOLLECTIONS OF A LORETTE.

I HAVE often met in the corridor of the *Pistole* a handsome young woman, with brown complexion and sparkling eyes. She is always gay, and there is something of mockery in her smile. Her name is Léa, and she is imprisoned here on a charge of swindling. She is said to have the intelligence of an angel, and the effrontery of a demon. I expressed a desire to see something of her, and was shown to her cell.

I found her seated at a little table sewing. She rose on my entrance, and did the honors of her cell as though it had been a drawing-room. I took a seat before a little earthen stove, in which a bright fire was burning, and asked if she felt unhappy in St.-Lazare.

"The days are very monotonous," she replied, "and, in a long stay, one might die of spleen. Fortunately for me, however, my recollections afford my mind sufficient distraction."

"Recollections of what?"

"Of my past exploits."

"They are sad ones, I think, since they conducted you to prison."

She replied, with vivacity:

"Not at all, madame; on the contrary, my life has been a very brilliant one, with entire liberty to do as I pleased, without let or hinderance from any one, and in the enjoyment of every luxury. I have had laces and jewels in profusion, and a table elegantly supplied, for the old wines flowed into gilded cups; blooded horses conveyed me to all the *fêtes* in Paris; a full share in all the pleasures within reach, and a smiling welcome everywhere; this *is* life. Were it all to last but a year, still, one might then say, '*I have lived.*'"

As she spoke, she threw aside the work in her hand. With a mortified feeling, I looked at her, and said:

"But this luxurious style of living—has it not cost you very dear?"

"Cost *me!*—nothing. Other people's fortunes went for it all."

Seeing that I frowned at this reply, she only burst into laughter, and continued:

"Madame, why do you compassionate men who are fools enough to let themselves be robbed by a woman like me? . . . That reminds me of the vicomte. That dear vicomte—didn't I finish him, though?"

"What do you mean by that?"

"Why, that I have ruined him, broken him up. A *roué*, a coxcomb, a blackguard, what you please; but Heavens! the handsomest man in Paris. In fact, I was told, until I was tired of hearing it, that the women all adored the Vicomte Maximin de ——."

At the mention of that name I started, as I thought of poor Valentine. She observed my emotion, and asked me if I knew him.

"Personally, no," replied I, "but I have heard him spoken of. And you tell me he is a ruined man?"

"Completely ruined."

"You are mistaken; he has married a rich heiress."

"He was on the eve of marriage when I set to work to love him—after my fashion. Many a woman had been made wretched by this man. By his marriage, he was about to plunge into despair these poor, abandoned creatures. I resolved to break off his marriage, and I succeeded. The first time I saw him was at the opera, where I was attended by a Russian that I wished to rid myself of, as I had already emptied his purse, once filled to repletion with banknotes. Between the acts, one of my friends talked to me a great deal about the vicomte. After the play, as we were descending the grand staircase, she suddenly said to me:

"'There goes the fashionable Lovelace.'

"I looked at him with curiosity, and he and I were in fact thrown together by the pressure of the crowd, so that the lace of my white *burnous* became entangled with the buttons of his overcoat.

"After that, we encountered each other everywhere and at all hours, in the Bois de Boulogne, upon the boulevards, walking, riding, at the theatre, and at concerts. In fifteen days from the time of my first meeting him, I received a bouquet from him, just as I was entering my carriage for a drive in the Bois de Boulogne. I laid the flowers on the cushion of the carriage. In one of the drives of the bois, the vicomte, on horseback, passed my carriage and saluted me. At this, I turned away my head, and threw his bouquet under the wheels of my *calèche.* The dandy stopped, stupefied, and bit his lips with vexation, but soon gave reins to his horse, and galloped out of sight.

"On my return to my apartments, I found his servant waiting for me, who had brought me another bouquet and a jewel-case, both of which I returned to him again. Whereupon, the vicomte became desperately in love with me, and determined to plead his cause in person. After I had kept him sufficiently long in a state of desperation, I accepted his first present: it cost him twenty thousand francs. Poor vicomte! I paraded him in public, and compelled him to give me his arm before everybody, and accompany me everywhere! To such an extent did I use my power over him, that the family of the heiress forbade him their house.

"When men cease to be tyrants, madame, they become weak and spiritless; then, we may ply them with the champagne they offer to ourselves, and intoxicate them with the love they fancy we possess for them. Meanwhile, they bedizen us with diamonds and rich toilets, for which they contract debts they can never pay. All his fortune was lavished on me—the chateau of his forefathers, his own house in Paris, until finally all his sources of revenue were swallowed up.

"One morning, he himself suddenly disappeared. When I leave St.-Lazare, I shall make the round of the various offices in the city, and I feel sure I shall find him at last, clerk to some notary in one of the faubourgs."

Here the young woman threw herself upon the bed and broke into loud laughter.

"Léa," said I, "you are highly intelligent. If you were only good, you would be called very accomplished."

"Madame," said she, rising from the bed, "I have been like a devastating torrent, a devouring flame. I am pitiless—I know it; but I am more logical than you. That man has snatched the crown of honor from the brow of the modest woman, and it is lost to her forever. In a moment of caprice, he has taken from her that which is dearer to her than life, and then thrown her aside like a broken toy. In the sight of God, and of Nature, we women are worth as much as a man, madame, and, since the laws they have made do not protect us, we must take justice into our own hands. Maximin has listened without pity to the sobs of his victims, and, as a woman, you can well afford to put up with the derision of his executioner."

As Léa stood up, with her eyes flashing fire, and her black hair in heavy plaits above her forehead, like a crown, there was something demoniac in her appearance. Instinctively I drew back. She perceived my movement, and said, with a smile:

"Are you afraid of me, madame? Fear nothing, I shall not insnare you; I am formidable only to men. Nevertheless, I confess to you I have had my day of remorse, and I applied myself then to the task of consolation."

The mocking expression of her face here disappeared, and, reseating herself, she continued:

"I remarked, among the circle of my acquaintances, a man quite *comme il faut.* He could drink his glass of champagne as well as another, and would laugh sometimes as though he wished to stifle reflection; but I often observed him with his eyes fixed on vacancy, and his head bowed in thought. I said to myself, 'He is unhappy, I must know the cause.'

"One evening, when my drawing-room was brilliantly lighted up and decorated with flowers, I passed my arm through his, and led him into my boudoir. I questioned him, and he confessed to me that he led an isolated life; that his daughter was in a convent, his wife had gone away on a journey, and that his empty house palled on him. The vicomte had just disappeared, and I was free. So, the very next day, I closed my house, sold my carriage, and installed myself with him in furnished apartments.

"At the termination of fifteen days' intimacy, it became my turn to be sad, which caused him to fear that I regretted the life of luxury I had led; and he proposed to me to reopen my former residence, and return to my gay *salons*, for he was rich enough to support the expense. 'No,' said I, 'it is simply a caprice of mine that makes me sad. I should like to live for one day in your own house.' After a thousand objections, he consented, having sent away his servants, under different pretexts, and we took our supper at his residence, where we were waited upon by new servants. My object was, to ascertain the secret of his unhappiness. For some time, perfect silence reigned at the table. I took care that he should drink freely, and, when the feverish gayety which precedes drunkenness had taken possession of him, I said to him:

"'Sir, what if your wife should return now?' I expected that uneasiness would replace his fictitious gayety. But his muscles never twitched. I resumed: 'And she is coming back, for I have made known to her how you are living.'

"He leaned back on his chair, and, raising his glass to a level with his eyes, replied:

"'No, madame, neither you nor any person besides myself has the power of bringing her back; for the walls of prisons securely keep those they hold.'

"I answered:

"'Sir, I fear the wine has crazed you. We were not speaking of a prison, but of your wife, who is at the springs.'

He slowly swallowed the contents of his glass.

"'My wife!' he exclaimed, 'what a sad story!

I always adored her, but she deceived me, and we have long been parted.'

"He covered his face with his hands, and tears streamed through his fingers.

"'She has left you, and gone off with a lover, no doubt?'

"'No, I confined her in St.-Lazare, myself.'

"'Do you tell me that you have shut your own wife up in prison?'

"'Yes. Poor Clemence! poor Marguerite!'

"'And who is Marguerite?'

"'My child. I have separated her from her guilty mother.'

"'And you tore your child from her mother's arms? I pity you, then, for you must have been quite sure of the mother's guilt.'

"'No, I am not entirely sure; at times, I even doubt if I was justified in doing as I have done.'

"'So, upon a mere suspicion, you have thrust your wife into the society of the prostitutes of Paris?'

"'Yes.'

"A long silence followed this response. I rested my elbows upon the table, leaned my head on my hands, and pondered deeply. The husband of Clemence said nothing more, but continued to drink. When he became lost under its influence, I ordered the wines and liquors removed, and bade the servant close the door after him.

"'Sir,' said I, 'this is a very amusing circumstance—a wife of yours in St.-Lazare! Do tell me about her love-affairs, and your own adventures; it will divert me greatly.'

"With incoherent words and maudlin expressions, he described, sufficiently for me to comprehend, the desperation of his wife's admirer, Francis, and the events of the last stormy interview of all three. I listened without interruption. When he had finished, he rose from the table, and conducted me with staggering footsteps into the drawing-room Withered flowers filled the vases, as they had been placed there on the birthday of Clemence. The master of the house extended his hand and touched them; this touch seemed to sober him somewhat. He leaned his head on the back of a chair, and sobbed.

"'No one,' said he, 'has set foot in this room since my wife left the house.' I regarded him in silence, and a crowd of busy thoughts occupied my brain. When his emotion had subsided, my plans were made up.

"'Sir,' said I, 'give me your arm, and let us quit this house. We will go and occupy my former *salons.*'

"The next day, I resumed my gay life. I bought back my carriage, and gave splendid *fêtes*, to pay for all of which he sold every thing he possessed, even to his wife's cashmeres. When he had nothing more left, he came to himself, and forsook me. A few days later, he went to the convent for his daughter, whose expenses he was now no longer able to pay. Thence, he went to St.-Lazare, and called for his wife. Placing the child in her arms, he said:

"'Clemence, I am poor now; will you pardon me, and return to me?'

She replied:

"'Since you have restored Marguerite to me, I will try to love you.'

"Clemence behaved nobly, and, finding that her husband was indeed poor, she has become entirely devoted to him. They have left Paris, and the daughter is being modestly educated and supported by the labor of the parents. They are happy, and I have reunited them—after my fashion."

I murmured to myself, "Poor Francis!"

"Do not be too much troubled about him," said she; "he has distinguished himself in the army, and lives in garrison in a remote part of France: ten years from now, no doubt, he will marry Marguerite." She ceased to speak, and appeared to be busy with her thoughts.

"Léa," said I, "what have you done with all the fortunes placed at your command?"

"I have spent them all, madame."

"And you have laid by nothing for the future?"

"No; what comes from the devil goes back to him again. I shall die in poverty."

"Then you have no thought of a possible old age?"

"Madame, people in my position continue young until, all at once, some day, we awake with the weight of a hundred years upon us."

She looked at me with an expression of melancholy, and continued:

"Madame, have you ever visited the hall of the *volontaires?*"

"Yes."

"And what were your impressions?"

"It is a painful place to visit. It is on the ground-floor of the infirmary department of the second section, a long narrow room with fifty beds in it. Old age is there, but old age without dignity. There, one may see the end, in disgrace and abandonment, of many a career once as brilliant as your own. In exchange for a short term of mad, joyous pleasure, one witnesses there faded beauty, premature decrepitude, a despicable old age, and often a death of despair."

She bowed her head, and said:

"I shall die in the infirmary of the *volontaires*."

"Léa," replied I, "you are still young; why not abandon the life you lead?"

"It is no longer in my power."

"But have you always lived thus?"

"Oh! no, madame, one is not born a *lorette:* I have a husband, who married me for my fortune, which he made use of to beautify his residence, and enlarge his business. He then installed me behind his ledgers, while he himself expended his income on women such as I have become. For a long time, I was in doubt about the facts; but finally the proof of his abandonment of me was too plain. Had Heaven granted me a child, perhaps I should have endeavored to bring the father back; but I was alone, and I did not attempt to mend matters. I am too proud to be made a victim of. So, one day, I closed my account-books, and, under the protection of a stranger, left the business. My husband was willing to part with his wife, on condition she left her fortune behind her.

"Madame, marriage, the most important step one can take in life, is often nothing but a matter of traffic. The touch of gold is corrupting—yet, between husband and wife stands the agent of corruption, her dowry. Let the dowry" (as recognized in European law and custom) "be done away with, and then marriage will be a contract based on freedom of choice. Restore this freedom of contract, and marriage, as an institution, will regain its original nobility, and once more hold out hopes of mutual happiness to the contracting parties."

"Léa," observed I, "why, when you leave St.-Lazare, will you not return to your husband? You might still be happy."

She shook her head and replied:

"My husband has squandered my money, as I have squandered the fortunes of my protectors. He has been succeeded in business by a former clerk, an intelligent man, who will become rich, and who has just married a portionless young woman of honorable character. She had been entrapped into a *maison de tolérance*, and, escaping from it, took refuge in his establishment, where she obtained employment."

"What! Adeline?" I exclaimed.

"Yes, that is her name; do you know her?"

"No; but I know all her history."

"Well, madame, she sits at the same desk where my husband placed me the day after our marriage. She will be happy, for she had no fortune, and she married from choice. Her husband chose her for her virtue, and not for her money."

At this point, the door of the cell was opened, and a domestic entered, bringing Léa's dinner. She removed her sewing from the table to the bed, and, when the dinner was set out, I perceived it to consist of a *vol-au-vent*, a *terrine de foie-gras*, some fruit, and a bottle of Bordeaux. As this was not prison fare, it must be remembered that those confined in the *pistoles*, and the *prévenues*, have the privilege of sending outside, through the commissioners of the prison, for any kind of food they desire.

As I rose to take my leave, the young woman tossed off a glass of wine, and the melancholy which had overcast her features gave place to her usual animated expression. She accompanied me to the door, and, as I was taking leave, she said:

"Madame, in future, I beg you will refrain from condemning such persons as myself, for we have our sphere of usefulness in society."

"I am not so sure of that," replied I.

"I insist, madame, if you please—and you can see it for yourself—that we are instruments in the hands of God, with which, in His wrath, He scourges the wicked. We are the fruit of despotism, and, when tyranny disappears from society, the *lorette* will disappear also."

November 20th.

I can write but little, my dear friend, for my health is still failing. I have just read over this manuscript, and have come to the conclusion that it is very imperfect, owing no doubt to the fact that, in writing, I have merely followed the impulses of my heart. You will find my ideas imperfectly expressed; but, with one of your intelligence, a little reflection will develop my thought. From what I have written, I also conclude that I have a sincere affection for womankind. In fact, I have always been led to pass a severe judgment on those who do not love their sex. Meanwhile, if a man should chance to read this manuscript, he would do wrong to accuse me of injustice to *his* sex, so long as my aim has been to render the wife good and useful in her sphere.

I have inculcated principles of economy, and urged that woman should occupy herself with her household duties, and strive to render her home happy, for her children's and husband's sake, as well as make it attractive to her friends. I have urged upon her the necessity of industrious habits, and of frugality in the expenditure of money.

Above all, I have endeavored to show women the necessity of having their daughters educated at home, under their own supervision. If husbands really understood their own interests, and wished to place their happiness on a secure basis, they would use *their* endeavors, also, to make home attractive to their wives, by creating agreeable occupations for them.

What task can be sweeter for a mother than to occupy herself constantly with her children? The wife, left free by the withdrawal of her children from their home, is not in a favorable position for sustaining either the honor or the welfare of her family. The child at home is necessarily the safeguard of the mother's reputation.

November 24th.

I have heard from Valentine. She is still in the central prison at ——. On the expiration of some portion of the term for which she has been sentenced, application will be made for her pardon, and hopes are entertained that she will regain her liberty. She is resigned, but her heart often turns lovingly toward the green hills of her native Normandy, where André, ever faithful, still waits her coming, and, notwithstanding the past, intends to bestow upon her his name.

November 26th.

I am to-day very sick, Marie, and I am thinking seriously of leaving St.-Lazare, and even Paris, altogether.

December 1st.

Marie, I set out to-morrow; I am about to turn my back upon the dear inmates of the prison. Although they have given me much painful thought, I love them, doubtless *because* they have made me suffer. It may be that what I have witnessed of their miseries, and of their errors and crimes, has so weighed upon me as to hasten the progress of my disease, and shorten my path to the tomb. Should I die soon, Marie, promise me not to forget my unhappy prisoners: do not despise them, but rather protect them, and implore virtuous and wealthy women to assist them. Replace me, but never give my name to the public. I prefer that my solitary tomb should be watered by your tears alone. I ask only a prayer from the stranger who shall pass it by, and to be forgotten by the world besides!

. . . .

Thus ends the manuscript of my friend. . . . She went to inhale the health-giving air of the south of France, where the tuberose and the orange-blossom shed their perfume. By short stages, she passed through France, never resting until she reached the shores of the blue sea. As she journeyed thither, and began to feel the influence of a more genial climate, her health appeared to revive, but the amelioration was more apparent than real. My friend dwelt for some time near the Mediterranean. She loved to bathe her emaciated hands in the white foam which the tide threw up on the strand, but she wrote no more.

On the 24th of December, 1865, one bright and sunny day, while seated in her easy-chair before the open window, she fell asleep. On awaking, she exclaimed:

"Ah! I have seen my dear prisoners once more. A purple haze floated over St.-Lazare; angels were kneeling in the chapel; women of majestic presence appeared in the corridors; the sisters seemed to be beings transfigured; tears still flowed from the eyes of the prisoners, but they were tears of joy and of repentance; they were about to abandon their criminal paths, and were protected by the generous and influential of their sex."

Here, overcome by weakness, she paused to regain strength, and continued:

"During all my life, I have never ceased to utter and repeat a demand, which the sufferers of my sex have reëchoed far and wide, and which will one day make itself heard in thunder-tones. That it will be so heard, is the hope I carry with me to the tomb. Yes," continued she, with kindling eyes, and extended arms, "I demand for my sex, respect for the virtuous, pity for the fallen, and succor for the unfortunate!"

She ceased, exhausted, and life seemed ebbing fast, after this effort. Restoratives were applied, and her forehead was bathed with cold water, after which she opened her eyes, and, pointing to a desk, said feebly:

"Look in that."

A manuscript in many sheets was found within, which was brought and placed upon her knees.

"This," said she, in accents scarcely audible, "is for Marie. When I die let it be sent to her. She must now have returned to Paris."

Raising her eyes toward the beam of sunlight which penetrated her chamber, she added:

"I seem to see a white dove, which has gathered in its beak the tears I have shed over St.-Lazare—tears which will descend again in consoling dew."

These were her last words on earth. She kissed the crucifix, looked once more to heaven, and died, resting her hand on the manuscript of "*Les Condamnées de St.-Lazare.*"

I have received these pages, then, as a legacy impressed by her hand, when moist with the sweat of death; they have since been covered with my kisses, and blotted with my tears. After repairing to St.-Lazare, to cast myself upon my knees in the now deserted chamber where she labored, prayed, and suffered, I resolved to publish "The Prisoners of St.-Lazare," and to publish it without the change of a word—for the writings of the dead should be held sacred. If the work shall bring about the good anticipated by my friend, her memory is destined to be held in perpetual honor. She herself has passed away, unnoticed, like a humble flower of the field; but the truest glory for her, as for all of us, is that glory which irradiates the darkness of the tomb.

APPENDIX.

ASYLUM FOR PRISONERS DISCHARGED FROM ST.-LAZARE.

The Prison of St.-Lazare is well known to be the only one in Paris where females are confined. Women under arrest, and awaiting trial (*prévenues*), those tried and sentenced (*condamnées*), young girls sent for correction, and females already embarked in evil courses, constitute its inmates. They are divided into two distinct classes. Those who have been guilty of minor offences, or who are simply under arrest, form one class, and those who are proved guilty of serious offences the other. The former occupy the first section of St.-Lazare, the latter the second. Heretofore, this distinction has not been kept in view by the public, nor has either one class or the other been the object of any special provision at the period of liberation. Houses of reformation are open to fallen women, but there is none to receive those discharged from St.-Lazare, either from the first or second section. It is to supply this need that the above-mentioned asylum has been proposed, which is intended especially for a house of *preservation.* Its value in this respect is apparent from the fact that the discharged prisoners, finding themselves abandoned by all, return to St.-Lazare, not to enter the first section, but to take their place among the criminals of the second, and perhaps only to become confirmed in their wicked courses.

There is, in the life of every woman who has fallen into the hands of justice, a critical, nay, a terrible moment. Is it that of her arrest? of her entrance into St.-Lazare? or, may be when she is arraigned and found guilty? No; none of these. Those events must indeed leave an indelible impression behind them; but there is another ordeal still more painful before her, and that is, her final discharge from prison. We have seen women faint away on recrossing the prison threshold, and welcome their return to liberty with tears of anguish. Alas! that there should be such legitimate cause for sorrow—that a life returned to freedom should be so filled with bitterness! Ordinarily, the liberated one finds herself an outcast from her family. Her friends have abandoned her, her position in society is lost, and, having no home of her own, she is generally obliged to seek shelter in some lodging-house.

As the *détenues* stay but a short time in St.-Lazare, they can have earned but little money, or no more than suffices to defray their first needful expenses. The prison authorities furnish to the inmates nothing but bed-linen, and no personal clothing that is allowed to be taken away, and thus, after only a few months' imprisonment, those who are discharged necessarily leave the establishment in worn and dilapidated garments. The proprietor of the apartment which had been occupied by the prisoner before her arrest has, meanwhile, sold her furniture to pay the rent, or whatever might have been left has been scattered or destroyed. If she had been in business, her customers will have transferred their patronage elsewhere, and misery stares her in the face. She decides to go out to service, but she has no certificate of character to show, no references to give. Then it is, she clearly perceives the position she is in, and often there is no refuge for her but in the waters of the Seine, or at the "*Bureau des Mœurs.*" In view of this heart-rending situation, a very simple idea, and one that may have suggested itself to the lady readers of this book, presents itself to the mind: which is, the opening of a house where these homeless women may be received for a time, and where they may obtain shelter, food, and clothing, and, thus finding means of support, they may be preserved from immediate danger. We desire that this house should prove to the inmates of St.-Lazare, sick in soul, what the Asylum of Vesinet is to the sick in body, when they leave our hospitals—*a house of moral convalescence;* that it may be a place of transition from the prison to the world again, where the inmates may have an opportunity of purifying themselves by repentance, and of strengthening themselves in their good resolutions; and where, treated with kindness, they may forget their debasement, and learn to respect themselves; a house where they will learn to love that society they have heretofore hated. Here they will gain a livelihood by their own labor, and will be qualified to support themselves respectably hereafter. By due attention to the laws of health as here enforced, they may repair their enfeebled physical forces, and be better prepared to maintain moral dignity in their intercourse with the world to which they are about to return. We hope, at no distant day, when our means shall permit, to have place in this house not only for discharged female prisoners, but, in a division by themselves, for all women who may be without homes and without work, and who are now obliged to seek either one or the other at St.-Lazare.

Extracts from the Rules for the Government of the Institution, adopted February 5, 1870.

Article I. An establishment is hereby founded as a house of preservation or employment for the discharged prisoners of St.-Lazare. It will receive a special designation when it shall have been opened for use. There will be admitted into this house—

1. Women who, having been arrested or sentenced to punishment by the correctional police, will find themselves, after their discharge from prison, without a home, and will thus be exposed to the danger of falling into immorality.

2. *Insoumises repentantes*, women guilty of irregularities of which they repent, and whom it is desired to save from registration, as professional characters, at the "*Bureau des Mœurs.*"

3. Young women who, being temporarily without asylum or resource, are subject to be arrested and sent to St.-Lazare, having no visible means of support. These women shall be divided into three distinct classes, as follows:

1. Discharged prisoners, whether *prévenues* or *condamnées*, who, after reformation, shall either be returned to their families or be placed at service in Paris, under the surveillance of lady patronesses.

2. Young *insoumises* (those unregistered) who, after changing their lives, shall be sent free of expense to Algeria, to a house especially prepared for their reception, and where their future interests will be cared for. As to females who may apply for a temporary home (the third class), they will leave the house as soon as work can be procured for them elsewhere.

Art. II. In order to accomplish the end in view, a house shall be bought or rented, which shall be furnished with beds and all other necessary furniture. All expenses of persons admitted to the house shall be defrayed by means donated, until the proceeds of the labor performed at the institution shall afford sufficient revenue.

Art. VI. The affairs of the house shall be managed by an administrative council of gentlemen, who will have charge of all matters of finance, litigations, etc., and the interior affairs of the house will be under the care of lady patronesses.

Art. XI. The lady treasurer shall keep all business documents connected with the institution open to examination. Every receipt shall be detached from a book which shall present its duplicate. An account of receipts and expenses shall be open to the inspection of all contributors to the institution, and of all agents of the civil authorities.

This undertaking in behalf of the discharged prisoners of St.-Lazare should not be the exclusive work of one person; it should enlist the coöperation of all. It should be sustained by the mite of the poor, as well as by the ample contributions of the rich. If society has its evils, it should know how to repair them, and valiantly carry the requisite burdens. We therefore call upon all true and noble-hearted women, and upon all men charitably disposed, to aid us, by every means in their power, to found this house of moral convalescence. We ask not only their charitable offerings, but, above all, their moral coöperation, as well as their sympathy and pity for our liberated prisoners, that henceforward the latter may have one place in the cold world where they may be allowed to repent and reform.

All persons desirous of coöperating in this undertaking are requested to address Mlle. Michel de Grandpré, Directress of Work, at St.-Lazare, or Mons. Honoré Arnoul, General Secretary, 44 rue des Batignolles. All donations to be sent to Mme. Frédéric Dollfus, Treasurer, 45 rue de Chabrol.

THE END.

www.ingramcontent.com/pod-product-compliance
Lightning Source LLC
LaVergne TN
LVHW010243110826
845151LV00004B/1379

* 9 7 8 1 4 2 5 5 2 3 8 7 9 *